SIPA ODYSSEY

BY
DORUSHKA MAERD
(Dharma)
(Now) A PHOENIX JOURNAL

SIPAPU ODYSSEY

ISBN 1-56935-045-0

Second Edition Printed by

PHOENIX SOURCE PUBLISHERS, Inc.
P.O. Box 27353
Las Vegas, Nevada 89126

March 1995

FOR INFORMATION CALL:
1-800-800-5565

Printed in the United States of America

COPYRIGHT POSITION STATEMENT AND DISCLAIMER

The Phoenix Journals are intended as a "real time" commentary on current events, how current events relate to past events and the relationships of both to the physical and spiritual destinies of mankind.

All of history, as we now know it, has been revised, rewritten, twisted and tweaked by selfishly motivated men to achieve and maintain control over other men. When one can understand that everything is comprised of "energy" and that even physical matter is "coalesced" energy, and that all energy emanates from God's thought, one can accept the idea that the successful focusing of millions of minds on one expected happening will cause it to happen.

If the many prophecies made over thousands of years are accepted, these are the "end times" (specifically the year 2000, the second millennium, etc.). That would put us in the "sorting" period and only a few short years from the finish line. God has said that in the end-times would come the WORD--to the four corners of the world--so that each could decide his/her own course toward, or away from, divinity--based upon TRUTH.

So, God sends His Hosts--Messengers--to present that TRUTH. This is the way in which He chooses to present it, through the Phoenix Journals. Thus, these journals are Truth, which cannot be copyrighted; they are compilations of information already available on Earth, researched and compiled by others (some, no doubt, for this purpose) which should not be copyrighted. Therefore, these journals are not copyrighted (except *SIPAPU ODYSSEY* which is "fiction").

The first sixty or so journals were published by America West Publishing which elected to indicate that a copyright had been applied for on the theory that the ISBN number (so necessary for booksellers) was dependent upon the copyright. Commander Hatonn, the primary author and compiler, insisted that no copyrights be applied for and, to our knowledge, none were.

If the Truth is to reach the four corners of the world, it must be freely passed on. It is hoped that each reader will feel free to do that, keeping it in context, of course.

TABLE OF CONTENTS

CHAPTER	PAGE
DEDICATION	1
TUE., OCT. 3, 1989	1
FORWARD	3
THE REDTAIL	8
PLATE I	9
PLATE II	10
THE PROTEST	11
THE "ACCIDENT"	16
RESISTING DEATH	18
TO HERE	21
PLATE III	27
PLATE IV	28
GLORIOUS DEATH	29
SPACE BROTHERS	36
GLORIOUS LIFE	44
PLATE V	52
THE RAINBOW BALLET	53
SMALL REVELATIONS	58
PLATE VI	61
ANCIENT REVELATIONS	62
FUTURE REVELATIONS	64
PLATE VII	67
PRESENT REVELATIONS	68
PLATE VIII	76
OPENING THE GATHERING	77
MOTHER EARTH AND THE ANCIENTS	84
THE MASTERS SPEAK	91
THE SPACE BROTHERS SPEAK	98
THE SACRED CIRCLE--THE CHRIST	105
CLOSING THE GATHERING	107
MIRACULOUS RESCUE	108
PLATE IX	111
FROM HERE?	112

BOOK INFORMATION, THE WORD, AUDIO AND VIDEO TAPES & ORDERING INFORMATION (at end of JOURNAL)

DEDICATION

REC #1 HATONN

TUE., OCT. 3, 1989   7:30 A.M.   YEAR 3, DAY 048

TUE., OCT. 3, 1989

TO MY SON, PAUL, WHO WAS GIVEN TO KNOW TOO MUCH AND UNDERSTOOD TOO LITTLE. PAUL MOVED INTO A HIGHER DIMENSION ON MARCH 22, 1985. NOW, OVER FOUR YEARS LATER I, TOO, CAN UNDERSTAND FOR HE LEFT US WITH A DIRECTION AND A PURPOSE BEYOND THAT WHICH WE COULD SEE WITH THE EYES.

AND TO SPOTTED EAGLE/LITTLE CROW, LAKOTA SIOUX, OF THE ANCIENTS WHO POKED AND PRODDED, NUDGED AND FINALLY DEMANDED THAT I DO MY JOB. I KNOW THE GREATEST ODYSSEY HAS BEEN THE JOURNEY SINCE THE DAY HE CALLED ME INTO MEETING AND SAID GO WRITE WHATEVER IS GIVEN UNTO YOU FOR IT IS YOU WHO MUST WRITE THIS STORY.

AND TO MY BELOVED HUSBAND, E.J., WHO THEN MADE IT LEGIBLE. IT WAS TO BE A SHORT MOTION PICTURE STORY LINE WHICH WE NOW PUT TO PRESS TO PRESERVE THE MANUSCRIPT. IT WILL ALSO BE A MOTION PICTURE.

AND TO ONE, SISTER THEDRA, WHO IS ALMOST NINETY YEARS OF AGE, AND WHO I DID NOT KNOW AT THE TIME OF THE WRITING, ALTHOUGH SHE IS NAMED WITHIN THE STORY. I DO NOT UNDERSTAND IT ALL, BUT I NOW DO KNOW THE TRUTH OF IT.

AND TO THOSE BLESSED ONES WHO GAVE UNTO ME THE STORY AND ACTUALLY WROTE IT FOR ME, I AM MOST HUMBLE IN THEIR PRESENCE, FOR THE GIFTS

OF TRUTH AND KNOWLEDGE GIVEN TO ME SINCE THAT TIME HAS BEEN INFINITE AND BEYOND MY COMPREHENSION. MY HEART OVERFLOWS WITH MY LOVE AND GRATITUDE THAT I MIGHT BE CHOSEN TO BRING FORTH SUCH OVERWHELMING SUBSTANCE UPON AN EARTH PATH.

I HAVE SORROW AND WEEP FOR THOSE ONES WHO WERE PRESENTED WITH THE GIFT OF GIFTS TO PARTICIPATE AND DID NOT SEE THE TRUTH OF IT. MAY THEY BE GUIDED IN THEIR UNDERSTANDING FOR THIS WAS ONLY THE BEGINNING OF A FANTASTIC ODYSSEY OF TRUTH BEYOND OUR COMPREHENSION.

I AM HUMBLY GRATEFUL TO COMMANDER GYEORGOS CERES HATONN, OF PLEIADES, WHO HAS SPENT THOUSANDS OF HOURS WITH ME SINCE THE WRITING OF THIS STORY, IN RELENTLESS TRAINING.

LASTLY, BUT MOST ULTIMATELY, I THANK GOD, ATON--THE CREATOR SOURCE AND ESU "JESUS" IMMANUEL SANANDA, WHO DO NOT LEAVE MY SIDE FOR THE WORD MUST GO FORTH IN THESE DAYS OF TRANSITION. I LIVE IN TWO DIMENSIONS; I ONLY PRAY THAT MY WORK MIGHT BE PLEASING UNTO *HIM*! TO THEM, I AM "dharma".

dorushka maerd

FORWARD

I am Hatonn, cohan of this chela (teacher of this student). Much in the life journey upon the placement of Earth must be understood in segments of Truth which pierce the veil of your memories, each and all of you who walk this trail.

This portion, which comes in fantasy format is, in fact, Truth in every measure--names have been changed for security of living individuals who would be removed from your life dimension were they located too soon. As Truth comes forth in segments ones can comprehend and accept it is most dangerous for those who dare to speak out. The life of this chela has been taken three times just since the writing of this "fantasy" and we have recommenced her life stream.

We of the Brotherhood of Light, and we who serve in the Intergalactic fleets and Cosmic Federation Councils, come forth to bring you knowledge for a most eventful and confusing transition into change. The time of your projected "Revelations" is upon you and we are sent from our Higher Sources to assist you and bring instructions for this final act of your play of third dimensional experience.

It was decided that we would first bring forth an "acceptable" story line that would bear a particular message to the ones awaiting instructions and the knowledge that the time of final instructions and "countdown" is at hand--it most surely served its purpose and we honor all of you ones who saw and heard the message and responded instantly.

It comes forth as a "fantasy" that man in mass can accept of the story as fiction but the heart will know of the Truth. Then, we can move on into the Truth of the instructions. Further, the entire story has not been enacted in your reality--but the Truth is there to its smallest detail. So be it.

I can only urge you ones who come into the gift of this small booklet, nudge yourselves into obtaining the information which has been presented in these past two months of 1989, for the veil is coming off and the curtain of Truth is rising most rapidly. Your proof of the Truth is all about you, in every corner of your planet. THE TIME IS AT HAND.

No Cosmic Brothers come to you in hostility for *if* you have attained a higher dimension with ability to travel through the cosmos--you do not live in such darkened transgressions as does Earth human. We come forth to discount the directed bombardments of lies which are perpetuated to terrorize you. We come hand in hand with God and totally in HIS service and service unto you that you can find your way, for you are lost and frightened. Please take of the hand extended unto you that we might give you benefit, for as you have petitioned God so has he responded in this manner.

There will be trials and tribulations beyond that which you can imagine but the way will be shown--the path cleared. We are come to bring you home to the Father's mansions--those who will come into knowledge. We bear no *"religious"* doctrines, for that is the bigotry of human, not cosmic Truth who knows no creed, color or separation of man from man. IT IS A JOURNEY WHICH WILL NOT BE MADE WITHOUT OUR PARTICIPATION FOR THAT IS THE PREPARATION PROMISED UNTO THE ONES UPON THIS ORB.

I will give no credentials for myself, at this time, for I do not wish to divert attention to anything controversial nor contentious in matter. Read with love and an open, flexible mind and Truth will come within. My credentials can easily be accredited through subsequent writings where that can be documented in your Earth boundaries of research.

If you find nothing else in this book, you will be reminded that your world borders on destruction and that life of soul and purpose of soul journey is forever--infinite! WHAT YOU DO WITH YOUR JOURNEY IS YOUR FREE-WILL CHOICE FOR THE DECISIONS WILL NOT BE MADE "FOR" YOU-- NO MAN CAN MAKE THE CHOICE FOR ANOTHER, YOUR BROTHER CAN ONLY HELP YOU FIND THE

PATH. THE PROMISE OF CREATOR IS BEYOND TIME, SPACE OR PLACEMENT. SO BE IT AND SELAH.

THESE THINGS SHALL ALL COME TO PASS IN THE TIME OF THIS GENERATION UPON THESE LANDS AND FOR THIS HAVE THE ANCIENT TRIBES RETURNED AND HAVE YOUR DISTANT BROTHERS GATHERED--OH YES, BROTHERS, THE EAGLES ARE GATHERED--WHERE WILL <u>YOU</u> BE?

Truth is being brought forth that you can prove unto yourselves that what I bring unto you is Truth. What you do about it is your own choice of action. You are a most unhappy people who live in an existence of the LIE. We give you opportunity to lift yourselves from the degradation and limits of that lie, up through the addictions and that negative impact placed upon you by those who call themselves your caretakers for you, as a people, have been sorely deceived.

You have time to become informed, <u>really SEE</u> that which is about you and about to consume you and rise into action as the Phoenix through the ashes into the new. NOT "NEW AGERS"--INTO THE "NEW" AS IN TRUTH. DO NOT ERR AND FALL INTO THE TRAPS OF THOSE WHO CHANT AND WOULD GUIDE YOU BY FOOLISH MENTAL GAMES WITH YOUR VERY SOUL AT RISK. LOOK AROUND YOU AT THAT WHICH YOU HAVE MANIFESTED INTO MATERIAL SUBSTANCE AND IS NOW DEVOURING YOUR VERY SOULS AND PHYSICAL BEINGS. YOU HAD BETTER BEGIN TO HEAR WHAT THE GOD OF SOURCE IS TELLING YOU INSTEAD OF SOME SELF-APPOINTED GURU WHO HAS MADE HIMSELF A SPOKESMAN FOR GOD--INSTEAD OF GOD. IT IS *JUST YOU AND GOD, BROTHER--<u>JUST YOU AND GOD IN THE ENDING</u>*!

This book was scribed some four years past, I write this on October 3, 1989 which in Truth is DAY 048 OF YEAR THREE. For you see, the ANCIENTS <u>KNEW</u> the Truth of it. The ancient calendars ended on August 17, 1987. YOU ARE ALREADY INTO THE FINAL DAYS OF TRANSITION.

YOU HAD BEST GET INTO HARMONY AND BALANCE WITH YOUR MOTHER EARTH FOR SHE IS MOVING, WITH OR WITHOUT YOU, INTO HER HIGHER BERTH FOLLOWING HER LABOR AND BIRTHING DELIVERY. 'TIS SHE WHO CALLS THE GAME PLAN FOR YOU ONES AND IT WILL BE SHE WHO WINS THE ULTIMATE GAME--HUMAN BECOMES INCIDENTAL AND SO SHALL IT COME TO PASS IN YOUR TIME UPON YOUR PLACEMENT--WHETHER YOU LIKE IT OR YOU DO NOT!

Heed my petition that you see and hear for it is wisdom that looks into Truth and finds the pathway to deliverance from the befuddlement--it is the foolish who disregard the final lifeboat and discounts the final trumpet call.

You can rise with the Redtail eagle into infinity or you can take the journey through the mire--the choice is yours.

I give honor unto one passed from your dimensions, WINDSINGER *Gary Smith*, who was given to pen the music which shall be utilized in the writings and motion picture production of I AM THE REDTAIL and BIRDS FLY AROUND HER. I will say no more at this writing for his property is most carefully guarded. He honored God for his gifts and we honor hm for sharing those gifts.

We also humbly honor Nick Eckert, who has contributed the sketches which are herein integrated, for they are from his own visions, contributed in storyboard format and are only a tiny portion of simple illustrations which might make the perusal of the document more enjoyable. Nick spent years in the art production of that which you labeled "STAR TREK". He has been given his own visions of Truth as to the evacuation and additional manifestations which shall occur upon your placement. We honor him for his participation and his willing offer to share the labors when the time is appropriate for the actual filming of the story.

We further honor one Wally Gentleman, who has clasped the vision unto his Truth and shall be given the honor (and the most burdensome) task of bringing forth this story in picture form which will grasp the heart of the masses. He is a most diligent, dedicated and questioning leader who demands perfection of himself and input from us of the higher planes. His shall be the glory of new innovations and a sharing personally with us of the Federation Fleet, for we have great technology to share in this visionary production of excellence. He has been a great contributor of new technology in your motion picture industry, and through greed and avarice of producer and director of a most innovative and conceptual motion picture, was deprived of honor and recognition of a most revolutionary concept in special effects--2001, *A SPACE ODYSSEY*, in my own humble opinion, the only really wondrous portion of the production. One day man of Earth will learn not to steal another's property for in so-doing, man diminishes himself to the lowest level of self accomplishment. That which is hidden, stolen in darkness, and is most secretly perpetrated upon your planes, is open and glaring in the higher places of the universe and will always eventually "*out*"--*for that which is sowed is cycled back into the reaping thereof.*

We dedicate this "Truth" unto all of you who will pick-up the dream and walk with us that we might fulfill our mission.

I am Commander Gyeorgos Ceres Hatonn and I salute you who allow me into your presence that I might make of this statement. We do not come in hostility; we come in love and brotherhood for you are in most grave circumstance, little Earth brothers. So be it and Salu.

I AM HATONN

THE REDTAIL

Dawn was hardly awake as the hawk took to the air for his morning ritual to the day. He was the Redtail, flying high above the world; down below him there was beauty; up above him there was beauty--there was beauty all around him. He greeted two ravens with a shrill shriek as he glided past them in his upward spiral.

Shortly he was joined by a second Redtail; they glided in tandem for a while, then one dove out of formation to rejoin Grandmother Earth. The lone hawk continued his journey to make sure his world remained unchanged from the day before.

He drifted over untold expanses of beauty, up canyons of crimson cliffs, over springs surrounded by trees; he sailed carelessly over stone formations which looked like moonscape goblins. He glided over beauty that only God could have painted on this canvas of Earth. He swooped up canyons where the Ancients had been in countless centuries past, and had left their paintings upon the cliffs to tell their secret stories until the end of time.

As the gliding master of the sky sailed up a river and soared over a roadway lying deep within a timeless canyon, he paid careful attention to the scene being played out below him.

Two cars were in the canyon; one a convertible holding three people, the other, a large black limousine which also contained three persons. The convertible was being pursued by the larger vehicle. The obvious intent was that of forcing the convertible from the highway. The larger vehicle rammed the convertible mercilessly until the driver of the convertible lost control of his machine and it burst through the safety rails and flew into the air off the roadside--to inevitably be drawn back to the Earth with lethal impact--"Oh, how wonderful to be a Redtail--!!!

The Odyssey had begun.

PLATE I

PLATE II

I AM THE RED TAIL

(Words to the Song)
(By Gary Smith)

I am the Red Tail
Climbin' and soarin' through your sky,
With the sunset on my feathers,
With your friends, all gettin' high!

Higher than the Red Tail,
Up above me, there is beauty all around.
Out beyond me, there breathes beauty.
Down below me, there grows beauty.
There is beauty all around me!

Learn to see me,
Learn to feel me, like the wind across my wings.
Let me spirit grow within you.
Learn to know me,
Learn to be!

Like the Red Tail,
Catching currents, and rising in the sky.
Out away from all that's ugly,
Breathing freedom from the windstorms,
Growing wise and filled with light!

You can be the Red Tail
A sunrise, a burst of glory in the sky.
You'll know freedom,
You'll know beauty,
You'll find love, and you'll be wise!

Rise with the Red Tail!
Strive to find, all the beauty in your Life.
Like the Red Tail you caught at sunset,
Like the Red Tail of your mind!

I am the Red Tail,
Climbin' and soarin' through your sky,
With the sunset on my feathers,
With your friends all gettin' high...all gettin' high...
all gettin' high.

THE PROTEST

It was a cinerama morning, not unlike millions of other days that had begun with spreading rose and golden rays across the same spot, on that very desert floor, for eons past. It was a morning best described as a watercolor or colored crayon morning with variegated rainbow hues of light in the east. A few drops of early moisture on a lone cactus flower at Bob's feet, waiting to vanish as the sun would spread more warmth across the landscape, caught his thoughts for a moment as he stepped from his convertible. He knew he would need to raise the top against the heat within an hour. It was early August and summer heat still claimed the Nevada desert. "Everything is the same, nothing is the same", flitted through his mind as he surveyed the panorama which spread in endless distance before him. For a brief moment even the wind had ceased its endless screaming and the Earth was stilled as if waiting for the next act to begin.

As he looked around he honestly wondered if there would be a turn of the century. Everything had changed. Weather patterns resembled nothing in recorded history. Earthquakes occurred where historically there had been none; torrential rains flooded rivers and streams where rain had previously been rare; temperatures ranged many degrees higher in summer and winters grew increasingly colder and more severe; as discernable seasons, spring and fall had disappeared. Drought destroyed areas previously excellent for natural agriculture while deserts experienced rains in torrential downpours; volcanos erupted which had been dormant for thousands of years. He had a premonition of some demented giant beast of prey.

He interrupted his thoughts as he turned and strolled toward a small group of people gathered at the main gate to the Nevada Yucca Flats Testing Grounds. He expected to find hundreds of people there attending a massive anti-nuclear demonstration. instead there were only a few standing around in detached small groups involved in private discussions. The event was to have begun two days earlier so it was apparent something had happened to change the plan. He would have to ask some questions but he was pretty sure he already knew what had occurred.

Bob had made arrangements with his closest friends, Steve and Diana Hensley, to join them for the demonstration/rally there at the main gate but they were no where in sight. Bob lived in Los Angeles awaiting sale of his house; following the sale he would be moving to the Tehachapi Mountains in the Mojave Desert area of California where he would join Steve and Diana who had made the move a couple of years before. The current plans were for Bob to drive to the rally, after tying up some business loose ends, and meet the Hensleys at the demonstration.

Following years of struggle and fighting, the government was continuing with plans to bury nuclear waste from the U.S. nuclear power plants at Yucca Mountain. The mountain was within the Yucca Flats test area so the federal government had total legal control. That particular waste material was the most radioactive substance on Earth. Even though several small earthquakes had rumbled through the Yucca Flats area in the past two years, the Feds had taken no apparent notice. Nuclear waste disposal had become by far the major problem facing not only the United States but the entire world. Bob knew he shouldn't expect the government to act otherwise; the problem was of such mammoth proportions that there was no workable solution other than closing down nuclear power production. The problem of disposal of the already existing waste would remain a major issue even if the "nukes" were shut down. Besides, nuclear (even hydrogen) devices continued to be detonated underground at Yucca Flats. The Feds made every effort to keep the information from the public but information leaks always occurred; the public was getting fed up. "At the rate man was setting up his own destruction in the United States, concern about some foreign country precipitating disaster was unnecessary," Bob thought ironically, to himself. What really struck terror to his heart, however, was what other countries might be doing with their nuclear wastes. In 1986 it was known that the United States ranked tenth down the list for use of uranium in nuclear power plants for production of electricity. France had ranked first. At that time it would have required a truckload of waste material every ninety minutes, twenty-four hours every day for twenty years, to deliver the nuke wastes for the U.S. to any one storage site. In the intervening time the problem could only grow worse.

What might the Europeans, Russians and Asians be using for storage of their nuclear wastes? That reservoir of death was guaranteed to be lethal for hundreds of thousands of years to come. Man was creating deadly time bombs which could be "triggered" for untold future generations, should we be fortunate enough to have future generations.

Bob returned his attention to the absent demonstrators. He was confident he knew where he would find them. The "Big Boys" had started to play rougher and rougher as the public became more and more vocal in their resistance to the damage to humanity and Mother Earth. People had begun to fight back and local police and local government agencies only half-heartedly cooperated with the Feds. No one in his right mind would want that deadly stuff in his playpen; surely no thinking person would want to live next door to one of those lethal disposal sites. Especially frightening was the detonation of hydrogen explosions mere feet from the buried wastes.

Bob and his friends always brought Travelers checks for two to three thousand dollars to all protest gatherings for use as bail money should it be needed. However, it had been a long time since any funds had been required. Facts were that law personnel and local residents greatly appreciated, and profusely thanked, the demonstrators. They extended every possible courtesy. Protestors were arrested and/or dispersed only because of direct Federal orders to do so. Arrest had become only a technical formality.

In addition to political "big boys" there were also ones jokingly referred to as "Mebies". "Mebies" was a short tag for "men in black" who were representative of "dark forces"; mafia/big business hoods who attempted to stop any progress toward what could be classified as "goodness and light". Somehow they sensed that the "love thy neighbor" idea would put them out of business. As Bob looked over the cars parked at the entrance he noted one of the "big black limousines" typical of the Mebies parked there. "Why would THEY be here?" flitted through his mind.

As he turned back toward the people at the gate he smiled a bit as he looked up into a gorgeous blue sky with only a few puffy clouds and made a mental note of the ever circling redtail drifting majestically overhead. At times he wondered to himself if there were only two on Earth. It seemed everywhere he found himself there would be one, and sometimes two, red-tailed hawks doing their graceful gliding ballet of freedom. He thought perhaps it might be the same ones. He knew better but it suited his fancy to claim one for his own. He liked to think of it as his "guardian angel" who could see all and know all, an entity untouched and undaunted by man's stupidity. "If I have my choice, I'm coming back as a redtail", he thought, "if there is a next time and if there's a place to come back to."

As he approached the group one of the men acknowledged his presence and, after exchanging a few pleasantries, he inquired about the happenings and whereabouts of the demonstration participants. As expected, the protest "leaders" had been arrested and taken to Las Vegas. The remainder of the crowd had been forcibly dispersed. The protest rally had, however, been successful. Many very well known public figures had attended and efforts had been effective. A restraining order had been handed down by the court to cease all test activities until further studies could be undertaken and evaluated.

Bob chose not to identify himself because the group remaining at the site was certainly not on his side of the issue. He and the Hensleys were among those having acquired dubious titles of "troublemakers" and the group within which he found himself was one against which he "troubled". He was unwilling to risk hostilities so pleasantly took leave of the group.

As he headed his car toward Las Vegas he pondered over his past twenty four hours. It seemed as if years instead of hours separated him from last evening. He had gotten too sleepy to drive safely so had parked off a side road, pulled out his sleeping bag and stretched out on the ground. He could mentally recall the fresh scent of the night-cooled, moist earth. He had stared at the universe above and felt overwhelmed by the Heavens. He loved to spend time in that manner and often went alone to the desert or mountains in order to spend a night under the stars. The experience always renewed his balance and refueled his energies. He had a strange attachment to those bits of light, as if he belonged out there among them. He had experienced such feelings and longings since he could recall memories. It was on one such night the realization came that he would do whatever would be required in an effort to bring a halt to the incredible "insanity" going on about him. He knew he could no longer leave the task to "someone else" but rather must make an active contribution to peace and safety on Earth. He had known from that moment he must pursue that goal regardless of physical consequences to himself. He silently thanked God that he was not alone.

It was about an hour's drive into Las Vegas and he knew where to go. This was his tenth trip to the local jail for the same purpose although he had usually been among the detained. He was filled with amusement as he entered the police station parking lot and stopped the car. The parking lot resembled a giant pep rally; the air was vibrant with victory and spirits were high. Local residents had brought large urns of coffee and boxes of rolls and doughnuts. His friends all talked at once in an effort to describe the happenings and express sorrow that he had missed the excitement. It was truly a fabulous day!

The demonstration brought much more rapid results than anticipated and that meant there would be some remaining time free for other activities. The participants had arranged to stay at the site for a minimum of three weeks should it become necessary. It was only Wednesday of the first week so there would be over two weeks to "vacation". Bob felt elated as he searched the sky for his "guardian redtail" and smiled to himself when he located it soaring in tandem with its mate in ever enlarging circles above. "Why," he asked out loud to the sky, "are you here? The jackrabbits are scarce in downtown Vegas. But thank you-- your dedication to Mother Earth keeps us reminded of our assignment to care for her."

THE "ACCIDENT"

Bob, Diana and Steve discussed the possibilities of some extended time for travel and a decision was reached to take the next couple of weeks and explore the Canyonlands of southern Utah. Steve had spent much of his youth at the Robbers Roost Ranch which at one time covered most of the area used by Butch Cassidy and the Sundance Kid as a hideout for the Wild Bunch. The ranch was located in a very remote and inaccessible area dotted with hundreds of ancient Anasazi campsites and ruins.

Bob had formed a close and lasting friendship with Steve while both attended college at the University of Utah in Salt Lake City. Bob had been to the Roost with Steve several times and it was exciting to think of returning for a few days. Diana had never been in that particular part of Utah so it was with much excitement that the three made plans for the trip. They decided they would leisurely drive along the route and stop for sightseeing as they wished. They made plans to rent a plane in Green River for an overlook of the ranch and canyonlands. They would then take enough extra time for a pack trip into the canyons. There were many ancient and beautiful Indian paintings in the canyons adjacent to the ranch as well as many old Indian ruins and caves to be explored.

Their immediate decision was to leave Las Vegas, drive for a couple of hours and spend the night in Mesquite, Nevada. They would also finalize their trip plans and make necessary phone calls.

Steve was driving as they left Mesquite the next morning and Diana was in the front seat beside him. They had hooked up the seat belts and Diana had snuggled happily as close to Steve as was possible considering the bucket seats and seat belts. Bob scooched over on his back across the back seat in order to soak in the beautiful sky and perhaps nap a bit in the warm sun. To anyone who might be following it would appear as if two young lovers were off on holiday.

As they entered an area called the Virgin River Canyon, traffic was light. The scenery was magnificent and moods were exuberant. An agreement had been reached among the three to discard thoughts and conversations of anything other than happy topics. They would simply leave all the nuclear negatives behind for the brief few days allotted for the vacation so they tittered happily about the adventures awaiting them.

Bob was napping when Steve became aware of a limousine rapidly approaching them from behind. Then, as the car slowed along side it became obvious that the intention was to force him from the highway. Steve made every conceivable maneuver in an effort to evade contact with the assailant and the minutes that followed were terrifying. Ultimately Steve could no longer maintain control of the convertible as he was being struck continually from his left by the much heavier car. Diana's door had flung open and only her seat belt held her inside the auto. Bob was being thrown about so violently that he finally was unable to get up from the floor where he had landed following the second impact.

The assault had continued for nearly a mile and they were deep into the canyon where the river was far below the highway in the bottom of the gorge. As the car left the road it ripped through a guard rail, flew over the embankment and crashed downward through brush and over rocks and boulders. the car finally came to rest more than half submerged upside in the river. Bob was thrown clear of the vehicle. His body lodged behind a shrub and very large boulder.

RESISTING DEATH

The limousine stopped, and three men peered over at the wreckage. They then hurried back into the still running auto and sped away when they noted an oncoming vehicle. The approaching car had been following farther behind the Hensleys and screeched to a halt at the break in the guard rail. The occupants had witnessed the accident from a distance, however they were unaware there were more than two persons in the convertible. There was a redtail hawk making tight circles above the scene, observing everything below. He screeched his piercing cry twice and continued his silent soaring.

Bob was only semiconscious and his body was positioned in such a way that he could only glimpse the foremost part of the car edged into the river. He could only watch helplessly as his beloved friends were overflooded by the water. He was vaguely aware that people had stopped to help, but was in such pain and helplessness he was unable to attract attention to himself. He sensed Steve and Diana were dead and had the perception that he, too, was dying. He could see that his left arm dangled half way to the wrist, and both arm bones protruded at an acute angle. Both his legs felt useless. Blood was pouring over his eyes from a cut on his forehead and his head hurt unbearably. Pain radiated from every pore of his body, and he wondered how long it took to die. The hawk continued to circle above the scene in its timeless way--forever observing. Bob had a remote feeling he was somehow with the hawk, or perhaps the hawk itself, looking down at the picture with total detachment. In the consuming pain he could only wish death would come quickly. It almost amused him to realize that he was thinking of death with cold irony. He and the Hensleys had accomplished so much in their recent efforts to better the environment and to do something toward healing Mother Earth, and here it seemed to bluntly end--in a river bed in an Arizona canyon. He wondered if this, after all, would be all there was to life. He was sure he would very shortly learn what if anything comes next after death and managed a half smile.

During the following period of time he was unconscious, and when he roused himself he could not tell how long his mind had been thankfully asleep. When consciousness would occur he was immediately swept away on another wave of pain. His awareness and desire to survive began, however, to take control during the periods of consciousness. He knew that in order to survive he must take some kind of action. With his one useable arm he was able to drag his body in slow, agonizing inches up the embankment. He moved toward a pitifully shallow spot of shade under a sparse bush. The unconscious periods seemed longer each time, but he knew he must retain enough awareness and strength to enable reach of the tiny spot of shade. He knew if he could not he would literally "cook" in the intense sunlight. In a final valiant effort he lunged forward, grabbed the root growth of the bush, and pushed and pulled himself forward. In the effort he lost his balance and rolled agonizingly over the broken arm and into a sandy washout at the foot of the bush. Blessed dark silence washed over his consciousness. As the darkness swept over him he was vaguely aware of the hawk. "Some guardian angel you are," he mused. He was not aware of the activity at the accident site and would have been only remotely interested anyway. Even in his lucid moments he felt removed from everything around him. As consciousness next crept into his reality it had been a longer interval of time in the unknown. He was again in full sunlight and the sun was much lower in the sky. He couldn't tell if he was dreaming or experiencing--the pain was his only connection with life. He tried to attach himself to reality, and he looked around as far as he could see without moving his broken body. He found that he had been able to pull himself into the mouth of what appeared to be a very deep canyon running perpendicular to the river gorge. To his right his eye caught sight of the hawk which had quit the air and was resting on a high rock ledge above him. He noted to himself that he was glad it was not a vulture or for sure he was in trouble. Looking in the other direction he focused, with extreme difficulty, on a shallow sandstone cave in the vertical wall of the side canyon. Blinking and staring he could make out a life-sized Indian painting. It was a picture of an Indian maiden with birds circling her head and shoulders. He felt he must be dead or dreaming--surely having hallucinations. The painting triggered a flood of memories causing him to realize that as long as he could use his brain and conjure memories he could maintain some attachment to reality. It also enabled him to evaluate the circumstances in which he now found himself.

He now became emersed in a scene in his memory of a day long, long ago when he had visited the Roost area. He had been hiking up a long forgotten canyon and happened upon an identical painting. He wondered if his mind was playing tricks on him but it seemed of no consequence, and of only mild interest.

As he roused following the memory experience of the painting, he realized that if he could keep his mind active with memories, he could sustain lucidity for longer periods of time. Therefore he thrust his efforts into recalling everything, even the most tiny details that entered into his consciousness.

TO HERE

It was natural that he began to reminisce about how he came to be in this place at this time. It all seemed to begin when Diana started to experience some rather strange phenomena. She began to have vivid psychic occurrences. Everyone chuckled about what she referred to as her "Angels" and "Spirit Friends". Although she told things with tongue-in-cheek style, it soon became obvious that no one should ever discount "Diana's Angels"; they were wonderfully accurate.

When the first big "gasoline crunch" occurred Steve had begun to dream of ways in which he might contribute to making America energy independent. The idea became his obsession and after several years of planning and research, he, Diana and Bob formed a partnership and started a small alternative energy company called Energy Alternatives. The original business thrust was in the cogeneration market but almost immediately the bottom fell out of that market because natural gas prices went up and the price paid for the electricity they produced was being reduced by the purchasing utilities. Things continued to fall apart in the alternative energy business; each project as it reached final contracts fell by the wayside for one reason or another. It always worked out that it was due to economic changes beyond their control but results were the same--disaster!

During this period of time Diana had begun to develop what seemed to be "far out" ideas. A couple of the children began to have unexplained experiences as well. In particular, their youngest son, Nick, became fanatical in his efforts to figure out how to reproduce some of the energy inventions of Nikola Tesla. He studied astrophysics in Colorado, and became almost a recluse in his tormented mind because of his fear of nuclear destruction. He was obsessed with the destructive aspects of pollution and toxic wastes. He was truly a man out of his time and could not compromise his values to those of current society.

Diana, on the other hand, felt an intense need to be able to contact "the sources" within her own mind and took time away from daily life to become a hypnotherapist. She became very successful in learning to contact her inner self and one day simply announced to the group that she had been told from "higher sources" that there was a great intended "mission" for the group and at the proper time the "Tesla secrets" would be given them. This would be in addition to many other instructions and information.

Just prior to his twenty-sixth birthday Nick killed himself. It was incredible how what appeared to be external influences seemed to ease the parents and family through the circumstances with almost studied stability. It was obvious, at least to the family members, that the boy had only ceased to exist in his tormented human state and moved into a more effective state as, what Diana referred to, a "Spirit Teacher".

Bob was in awe as he observed the happenings of the next couple of years unfold. Changes were dramatic in all members of the family, friend groups changed and directions became firm. Bob too underwent major changes within his own belief systems. Through Steve and Diana he met a Lakota Souix Medicine Man who became a dear friend and teacher. He was at last sorting out his own "roots" and liked what he found.

The death of Nick seemed to be a turning point of great magnitude. It was almost as if he had come to Earth for that purpose. Steve's response was profound and he immersed himself in efforts to further his understanding, love and peace. Bob had always discounted any reference to the possibility of reincarnation or pre-planned missions to Earth, but he was witnessing events that spoke otherwise.

After setbacks in the cogeneration portion of the business the company moved into the production of electricity via wind turbines. At that time the wind farms were established as tax shelters so the machinery was about as bad in most instances as laws permitted, and almost all of the wind turbines eventually failed. Energy Alternatives also failed along with many other companies in the energy industry during that period of time.

Groundwork had been set in place, however, how far back Bob couldn't guess, for events that would take place following failure of the company. It seemed that through guidance, which appeared to have no source except from other dimensions, business plans came forth which seemed inspired toward success. Financial opportunities began to tumble in one upon another. Opportunities opened up in areas in which, at first observation, there seemed to be no talent or affinity for participation. It was simply assumed that those things were intended and every opportunity was accepted with grace and appreciation.

Steve and Diana believed directions were being given them to become anonymous in their activities; the company was dissolved and they underwent personal bankruptcy so as to completely disassociate themselves with their unsuccessful past. They laughed a lot and lovingly referred to their projects as "God's work". They became very active in the movement toward enlightenment and help for humanity. Bob found it contagious and before he realized it, he too was up to his neck in the same activities. He loved it; he loved the people he met and was beginning to feel very productive along with gaining a much longed for inner peace. He often wondered what in the world people were thinking about when they cast stones toward those involved in trying to help their fellow humans and the wonderful Earth upon which all must live. After all, there can be no escape from the planet--if you go up, you have to come down; if you move outward, you have to come back. We are attached to Earth and it becomes clear that we must learn to treat our existence here more respectfully. We must nurture our "Mother" and stop our destructive games or, it is obvious, we will all perish.

One of the "instructions" Diana had received in a meditation was that a movie, or series of movies, should be made to alert the public to the terrible visceral damage being done to Mother Earth by the nuclear explosions, acid rain, toxic wastes and hydrocarbon pollution. Steve and Bob were directed by Diana to several books and writings, both ancient and modern, strongly suggesting that the Earth acted as a huge single electrical conductor. This hypotheses was completely in accord with the findings and research of Nikola Tesla.

The paramount meaning of that information wasn't clear until Steve and Diana spent several hours with Sister Thedra after the Second Annual Gathering of Light at Mt. Shasta. She showed them a recent drawing done through a scientific channel in Argentina which clearly indicated that the Earth has accumulated enough negative energy to create a latent tilt of thirteen degrees from its present axis. At the Gathering several of the channelled entities had made explicit references to the great concerns of the Mighty Council of the Intergalactic Fleet that they might be unable to support the present axis long enough for humanity to reverse the negative energy flow that was creating the problem. They had made it abundantly clear that all of creation is made of energy and that negative thoughts (of war, terrorism, hate and general human unhappiness) imputed a negative charge to Mother Earth which must be offset by positive thoughts (love, happiness and peace) to bring her into balance. Any nuclear explosion in space will result in the Fleet's removing their temporary balancing energy which will allow the shift of axis to immediately occur. The tidal waves, volcanic eruptions and earthquakes following such a shift would probably eliminate most life on the planet. Thus it became clear, especially to Diana, why the movie was so extraordinarily important.

Needless to say, the responsibility weighed heavily on both Diana and Steve even though they received the love and support extended through Virginia Essene and Ann Valentine who had published the two most valuable books available in those days, *Secret Truths* and *New Teachings*. The major pillar of strength was, of course, Carl Bryant, the Peace Pipe Smoking Sioux from South Dakota. He always had the right stuff at the right time for Diana, whether it was encouragement, laughter or a swift kick.

Bob roused himself briefly and then again lapsed into the semiconscious twilight to avoid the pain. His mind went back to his favorite memories of some fifteen years ago. It had been, all at the same time, the most difficult and yet wonderful time of his life.

He had been sent to Argentina on a business trip and found himself with a couple of weeks of free time. He had always had a nagging wish to go to Peru and see the ancient ruins of Machu Picchu and the Plains of Nazca. He had read of the giant engravings and phenomenon which was reported from that area; had read all the books about so-called space vehicles, and was aware that the Peruvians accepted, without question, the presence of space craft. At any rate, he had always wanted to investigate the area and took that opportunity to do so.

Early in his visit he met a delightful couple, Richard Peterson and his friend, Athenia. Athenia's friend, Anranjia, appeared the following day and Bob was totally captivated by her. They called her Ranjia and very soon the four were practically inseparable. Some of their stories seemed incredible to Bob and he only half believed most of them. Richard had told him that he, too, had not believed the stories as they were told to him--in the beginning. However, he changed his mind. Athenia and Ranjia simply stated they were here from another planet and proceeded to prove it. Richard had the opportunity of traveling in one of their shuttle craft and had taken to visit on one of the large ships called a "Mother Ship".

Bob had fallen hopelessly in love with Ranjia and, although she continually explained that she was not of the planet Earth, he never really believed it. She told him that she was here on a mission and would find it necessary to be available to depart at any time her orders were to do so. It came, however, with as much surprise as if he had never been told of such a thing when suddenly one evening she and Athenia announced that they would be leaving first thing in the morning. They said there was a crisis regarding Earth which necessitated massing of the space fleets. She had started to go into great detail but stopped when she sensed the heartbreaking conflict going on inside him. Too late he had accepted her honesty and the following day she, Athenia and their "space brothers" vanished.

Bob was devastated--totally lost. He knew in his heart there would never be another love for him. He stayed around Lima for a few days with Richard but knew he must return to Los Angeles and get on with his life. He had never stopped having her visit in his dreams.

He was musing in the painful pleasure of those Peru memories when the pain of the human body roused his consciousness. As he squinted through blurred eyes he saw the redtail sitting on a ledge above his head. It took flight, swooped low over him and glided up the canyon. It appeared to Bob that the hawk simply dissolved into the painting on the cliff face. His consciousness dissolved also.

As he roused again he looked up the canyon where the hawk had gone--the last thing he remembered was the vision of an Indian maiden standing on a boulder beneath the area where he had seen the painting. He made a desperate effort to hold on to consciousness but it slowly slipped away once again.

The maiden motioned to someone further up the canyon and four young Indian men moved quietly forward to join her. She ran over to Bob and began to evaluate his injuries. The men unrolled a travois, gently gathered Bob onto it, and as his darkness folded about him they were taking him gently up the canyon trail. All that remained were the drag trails in the sandy soil and the ever-watching hawk.

PLATE III

PLATE IV

BIRDS FLY AROUND HER
(Words to the Song)
(by Gary Smith)

Deep among the canyon walls, I hiked alone while silence
    flowed
In some cool shade I stopped to rest and drink some water.
Looking up, I noticed her, an act of love was painted where
The sandstone face slipped down to meet
    --the crumbled ages.

Unknown hands from years gone by, had stopped to rest here,
    the
        --same as I;
But with his brush and paints of clay, he left his love
    here.
A painted girl to greet the dawn.
A crown of white, a feathered gown;
Her smile demure, she waited while
    --birds flew around her

A thousand years this love has grown
    and stood the test of wind and storms,
While my love waits beyond these walls,
    --birds fly around her.

The canyons grown and canyons die, as sand dissolves behind
    her eyes,
Her painted birds will tumble down and join the ages.
The grass turns green and then to brown, a thousand times
    before her crown;
Although she's changing, slowly fading,
    --her love will live here,

So who am I to linger here?
I'm just a flash before her mirror,
A fading whisper who stops to watch
    --birds fly around her.

GLORIOUS DEATH

As the car submerged an energy became visible above the vehicle. It was Diana's soul essence which had departed her physical body as it had careened over the river embankment and crashed through the brush and boulders, still locked within the metal machine. Almost instantly her energy essence was joined by a second energy which emerged from the vehicle. There was instant recognition between the energies as they hovered above the scene displayed in the river. Both energies were aware they were departed from the physical bodies within the automobile but recognized no emotional attachment to the happenings below. They simply observed the activities with some amount of interest but total lack of concern. Both energies were aware of a total well being, infinite peace and overwhelming joy. They heard the voices of the onlookers with detachment and at the same time were free and floating as if on the waves of strains of beautiful music.

Both entities were aware of Bob's physical body as it lay broken against the rock and brush but felt no participation within the scene itself. They were aware that the energy entity known as Bob was still present in the human physical form that lay beneath them. There was no longer need of their presence.

They lingered momentarily to observe the activities one last time as if observing some far distant play being enacted on an illusionary stage. They witnessed the frantic activities of the helpers in their efforts to free the two collapsed bodies from the automobile. They made an effort to draw the attention of the onlookers toward Bob's broken body and found they had no way to communicate with the physical beings who were only inches from them. After observing the activities for a few brief moments they turned away to face whatever lay before them in this new awareness.

It was as if they were immediately immersed within what appeared to be a whirling tunnel of darkness. They were aware of entities present all around them as they traveled through the tunnel. At the distant end toward which they were floating was a brilliant light. The light seemed to reach out to them to draw them into itself. It was as if they, too, had become less dense. There was such overwhelming love and peace that all connection to Earth's physical existence was evaporated from their awareness.

As they neared the opening to the tunnel there appeared more entities which were easily recognized by each. Each was also aware of the presence of other energy entities which they could only describe as angel forms. The Light became more and more intense magnetically until they were thrust into the Light itself; they, too, had become light but not of such brilliance as that before them. The absolute love energy, for which the human entity has no description, completely engulfed them and dissolved them. They knew this love force could only be the God Love Itself. They had come home.

As they dissolved within the Light there was recognition of total knowledge. Every minute portion of existence, of all time and all dimensions, was instantly and concurrently comprehended. They had become all beings, all things in infinity. There was no beginning and no ending; there was simply "being".

Out of the vibrations of the Light itself came a voice which spoke to them. "I AM THE SOURCE OF ALL THINGS. I AM THE CREATOR OF ALL. I AM ALL! YOU HAVE PASSED FROM WHAT YOU HAVE KNOWN AS THE THIRD DIMENSION. YOU HAVE BEEN BROUGHT THROUGH THE SHADOWS AND VEIL OF IGNORANCE AND DARKNESS AND YOU HAVE NOW BECOME LIGHT. YOU HAVE ENTERED A MUCH HIGHER DIMENSION THAN YOU COULD HAVE EVER DREAMED OF IN YOUR HUMAN FORM. AS YOU EXPERIENCE THE KNOWINGNESS YOU MAY ALSO EXPERIENCE CHOICES REGARDING YOUR JOURNEY WHICH YOU PERCEIVE TO BE IN YOUR FUTURE. THERE IS NO TIME AND NO SPACE; THERE IS ONLY THOUGHT. THERE IS ONLY ILLUSION AND IT IS ONLY THROUGH MY THOUGHT THAT ENERGY COALESCES INTO WHAT YOU HAVE PERCEIVED AS MATTER. YOU ARE ALL; I

AM ALL. YOU ARE MY THOUGHT CREATION; THEREFORE YOU ARE SIMPLY AN EXTENSION OF MYSELF.

"THERE IS MUCH PERCEIVED NEED, MUCH SUFFERING AND PAIN ON YOUR PLANET EARTH. THAT WHICH YOU CALL MOTHER EARTH, THAT BELOVED LIFE ENTITY WHICH I CREATED, IS BEING DISEASED AND TORTURED BEYOND THAT WHICH SHE WILL NO LONGER ENDURE. SHE BORE YOU AND PROVIDED FOR YOU AS HUMAN ENTITIES UPON HER SKIN AND ATMOSPHERE AND YOU HAVE BROUGHT DESTRUCTION UPON HER INSTEAD OF LOVE AND HARMONY. HARMONY IS THE ULTIMATE GOAL IN THE UNIVERSE AND LOVE IS THE ONLY ROUTE BY WHICH THAT GOAL CAN BE REACHED. LOVE IS THE MOST JOYFUL OF ALL MY THOUGHTS SO I CHOOSE TO THINK IT THE MOST. YOU ARE PRECIOUS TO ME AS ALL OF MY THOUGHT CREATIONS ARE PRECIOUS TO ME.

"WHEN I CREATED THE HUMAN ENTITY AND GAVE HIM THE EMERALD PLANET EARTH UPON WHICH TO EXPERIENCE, I ALSO GAVE HIM FREEDOM OF WILL. MAN HAS USED HIS FREE WILL IN MANY NEGATIVE AND HURTFUL WAYS. HE WAS GIVEN CHOICES AND HE OFTEN CHOSE THE DARK PASSAGES AND BROUGHT HURT AND DAMAGE UPON MY OTHER CREATIONS. ALL MY CREATIONS ARE PIECES OF THE TAPESTRY OF EXISTENCE; EACH PIECE IS NECESSARY TO COMPLETE THE WHOLE. MAN HAS GAINED KNOWLEDGE OF TECHNICAL MAGNITUDE BEYOND THAT WHICH HIS SPIRITUAL GROWTH HAS MATCHED. HE HAS PLAYED WITH TOYS OF DESTRUCTION WHICH IF UNLEASHED CAN CHANGE THE VERY VIBRATIONAL ORDER OF THE UNIVERSE ITSELF.

"I DO NOT LIKE TO UNCREATE MY THOUGHT MANIFESTATIONS. I LIKE TO BRING MY THOUGHTS INTO EXISTENCE AND KEEP THEM FOR A WHILE AND ENJOY THEM. THOSE ENTITIES SUCH AS YOU BRING ME

GREAT JOY IN YOUR EFFORTS TO CLEANSE AND HEAL YOUR LIFE SOURCE. IT HAS BROUGHT SPECIAL JOY THAT THERE ARE THOSE OF YOU WHO ARE CEASELESS IN YOUR EFFORTS TO BRING TO A HALT ATOMIC DESTRUCTION. WHAT YOU HAVE KNOWN AS HYDROGEN IS A BASIC ELEMENT OF THE UNIVERSE ITSELF. PHYSICAL DEATH RESULTING FROM NUCLEAR EXPLOSIONS AND RADIATION OF THAT SUBSTANCE DAMAGES THE VERY FREQUENCY OF THE SOUL ENERGY ITSELF.

"AS YOU STAND HERE WITH ME WITHIN THE LIGHT, I GIVE YOU A CHOICE. EACH ENTITY HAS ITS OWN PLACE IN THE UNIVERSE SO EACH MUST, WITHIN ITS KNOWINGNESS, MAKE ITS SEPARATE CHOICE. YOU MAY NOT CHOOSE FOR EACH OTHER. YOU MAY ONLY CHOOSE YOUR OWN DIRECTION.

"THERE WILL BE MADE AVAILABLE TO YOU THE POSSIBILITY OF REMAINING IN THIS PRESENT DIMENSION WITHIN WHICH YOU ARE EXPERIENCING. SHOULD YOU REMAIN IN THIS PARTICULAR DIMENSION YOU WILL BE TAUGHT MANY TRUTHS. YOU WILL BE SHOWN MANY THINGS. YOU WOULD BE TAUGHT THESE THINGS SO THAT, SHOULD YOU RETURN TO YOUR THIRD DIMENSIONAL FORM--INTO YOUR EARTHLY HOUSE OF PHYSICAL HUMAN FORM, YOU MIGHT HELP YOUR FELLOW HUMAN TO FIND DIRECTION AND TRUTH. YOU WOULD RETURN AS A TEACHER AND LEADER TO FACILITATE THE REBIRTHING OF YOUR EARTH PLANET. SHE IS IN GREAT PAIN AND IT WILL ONLY BE THROUGH THE GREATEST OF LOVE AND NURTURING THAT SHE WILL BE ENABLED TO SURVIVE WITHOUT A COMPLETE CATHARSIS.

"TEACHERS AND GUIDES WILL BE PROVIDED SO THAT YOU CAN KNOW YOUR DIRECTION SHOULD YOU MAKE THE CHOICE TO RETURN TO THAT MORTAL

FORM. OR, YOU MAY SIMPLY CHOOSE TO PASS ON INTO THE HIGHER DIMENSIONS OF SPIRIT ENERGY.

"YOU RECOGNIZE THAT YOU HAVE PASSED THIS WAY BEFORE BECAUSE YOU HAVE. THERE IS ONLY NOW AND I KNOW THAT YOU ARE HERE AGAIN TO RECEIVE FURTHER INSTRUCTION. THE CHOICE IS YOURS. YOU MAY PASS ON TO HIGHER DIMENSIONS OR YOU MAY STAY AT THIS DIMENSIONAL LEVEL FOR THE INSTRUCTION.

"SHOULD YOU CHOOSE THE WAY OF THE TEACHINGS THERE WILL BE ANOTHER OPPORTUNITY TO MAKE A CHOICE OF REMAINING IN SPIRIT OR RETURNING TO THE MORTAL FORM. I AWAIT YOUR ANSWER. YOU MAY SIMPLY EXPERIENCE THE LOVE AND JOY FOR A MOMENT AS I FEEL YOUR JOY AND ECSTASY.

"I SEE THAT YOU HAVE MADE YOUR CHOICE; I WELCOME YOUR PARTICIPATION. YOU BRING ME JOY. YOU WILL RECEIVE KNOWLEDGE SO THAT YOU MIGHT RETURN TO EARTH IN ORDER TO BRING OTHERS TO AN UNDERSTANDING OF ME. SO BE IT.

"I HAVE SUMMONED GUIDES TO ASSIST YOU IN REACHING YOUR TEACHERS AND A PLACE TO EXPERIENCE THE LESSONS. YOU WILL RECOGNIZE THEM AS YOU HAVE KNOWN THEM BEFORE. I SUMMONED YOUR BROTHERS FROM WHAT YOU HAVE CALLED SPACE; FROM YOUR OWN SOLAR SYSTEM. THEY ARE SIMPLY YOUR OLDER BROTHERS WHO HAVE MASTERED TECHNOLOGY ADVANCED OF YOUR HUMAN KNOWLEDGE. DO NOT CONFUSE THEM WITH ENERGIES OF THE HIGHEST CAUSE; THEY ARE SIMPLY ADVANCED OF YOU EARTHLINGS AND ARE AVAILABLE AS ASSISTANTS TO RENDER AID AND ASSISTANCE IN THIS MOMENT OF CRISIS. I BLESS YOU."

As the ultimate brightness withdrew and what appeared to be a misty vapor evaporated, the energy forms of Steve and Diana took on the substance of material form.

From the distance three entities moved rapidly toward them. The entities were dressed in what appeared to Steve and Diana as "space suits". The suits were of metallic appearing material with close fitting form. Boots were formed so well that they appeared to be attached to the suits themselves. The foremost entity extended his arms in welcome and introduced himself as Yeorgos. He turned and introduced the other beings with him as Hypcos and Athenia. There were warm greetings amongst the group and a moment of utter surprise as recognition flashed through the group. There was instant knowingness that Diana had been one of this group of cosmonauts in some other moment of time. Steve, too, knew that he had experienced a like existence as the feelings were familiar and comfortable. He felt an overwhelming commaderie with these people.

Yeorgos told Steve that the present group originated in the Pleiades and one of the moons of Jupiter. Yeorgos explained that there was much activity taking place at the Galactic Fleet level as activities on planet Earth grew to crisis proportion because of the nuclear experimentation and detonations. He also explained that he was a commander of one of the space commands and that these were his fellow cosmonauts. He said he had been instructed to make them comfortable in their new surroundings. There was an immediate eagerness to share old memories and wonderful anticipation of learning new and different technology. It was as if all the Earth experience had become only a hazy memory. The movement from one frequency vibrational dimension to another always produced changes in the memory data banks. The memory, however, would always grow sharper in the higher frequency and what occurred while in a higher dimension would always be temporarily blocked when an entity returned to the lower dimensions.

They were located in an area very similar to the canyon in which they had been in the river. Gorgeous variegated crimson and gold cliffs of stone rose above them in the distance and they could look forward to a wide valley with trees lining a river bank. In one or two places water cascaded over the cliffs from above and joined into the stream bed in the valley. The view was magnificent. The Earth itself seemed to be dissolved from the stone in that it was all of such gloriously vibrant colors. The air smelled fresh and clean and the warmth of the Earth felt good against their feet. Occasionally they picked up the scent of burning wood wafting through the air. There was only a bit of breeze now and then and the temperature was mild and pleasant. The group chatted happily as they hiked along a well-worn path which ran beside the stream.

As they rounded a curve in the canyon a spectacular sight lay before them. The valley floor widened broadly and the scene left Steve and Diana stunned. Directly ahead and a bit to the right of the stream was a craft of breathtaking form. It was obviously the craft from which the cosmonauts had come. It gleamed in the sun like a giant silver disc poised to sail into the distant forever. Questions tumbled through their minds one upon another, too quickly to be expressed. They knew they would be given answers as would be proper but it seemed as if their mental circuits were somehow jammed.

As they moved toward the craft the scene took on proportions of total fiction. They had somehow been placed in a situation which appeared to be somewhere between reality and fantasy. Farther up the canyon, which continued to widen and bend somewhat, was an even more unbelievable sight. Before them were fields in which Indians were tilling corn and some type of grain. There were also areas of tilled land in which green vegetables and root foods were being grown. At the foot of the canyon walls were dwellings of adobe. Farther up the sides of the walls, in areas where the cliffs had long ago broken and fallen away, were tucked whole villages of ancient Indian dwellings. They had been placed in the midst of the ancient past which had somehow become the present. As they looked behind them at the spectacular spacecraft they knew that what they had perceived as the future was also the present. They knew that whatever awaited them would be "out of this world".

SPACE BROTHERS

As the five approached the spacecraft, Steve remarked that he had not seen the craft until they were quite near relative to where he felt it "should" have been visible. Due to its large size it should have been visible for a long distance, and he inquired as to why they had not seen it sooner. Yeorgos answered that there is an electromagnetic field around the craft which would cause it to be invisible when the field is activated. Once an individual's own personal vibration frequency was elevated, however, it would always be visible. He pointed out that Steve and Diana had made the transition into a higher dimensional vibration frequency which would continue to increase as they became more attuned.

As they entered the craft two people moved forward to greet them and Yeorgos introduced them. One was a tall man about six feet in height, slim and bearded. His beard was very well trimmed and was of a light brown color which matched the color of his hair. The man's name was John and he had a warmly glowing and gentle smile. Energy and love radiated from his presence. Diana was instantly drawn back to the feelings she experienced in the presence of the energy form within the light as they had emerged from the tunnel. Hypcos noticed the reaction and quickly spoke up in order to put the two at ease. He explained that John was an entity who had attained the ability to move intra-dimensionally. His creation had originated in one of the highest of dimensions and he had come to planet Earth specifically for the purpose of teaching. He would be working with them both to enable them to raise their personal vibrations to an even higher level. He was to be a guide from a high frequency spiritual aspect. Yeorgos added that the real value is in the spiritual aspect and knowledge and that the Space Brothers were to be only assistants and helpers.

The second man was not quite as tall and had very light hair and eyes. He was dressed rather casually, in an earthly manner. Yeorgos introduced him as Richard, and said Richard had a very interesting history which would be enjoyable to share. Richard had most recently come from Peru. Yeorgos noted with humor, that Richard was a fellow cosmonaut who had agreed to manifest on Earth planet for the purpose of awakening Earth brothers and begin early stages of enlightenment. Richard's frequency had zipped down near zero when he had passed into the lower density of Earth's atmosphere. Because of that he had wandered about rather aimlessly for years in Earth time. He had gone to Peru and the opportunity was correct for Athenia to join him and cause him to "remember" his purpose. Athenia and Richard had been "married" prior to the Earth escapade, so it was especially pleasing that she would be the one to work with him in Peru. Athenia and her comrades from outer space were based in the Andes Mountains at the time. Richard's mission was to "experience" from the aspect of a human and then write about those experiences. The information would further validate the existence of space brothers and accurately begin to establish their correct relationship. Earth man had a most heavy urge to make the brothers some type of God-being, and that misconception was to be corrected. Yeorgos was obviously enjoying himself very much at Richard's expense. Steve was sure that there would be some amusing stories regarding Richard's experiences as a human.

As the group arranged themselves on the cushions offered them, Athenia moved hers next to Richard and settled comfortably against his knees. Steve studied her intently; he had never seen such eyes as Athenia's. They were blue and yet, that didn't quite describe them. They were iridescent blue-silver and bottomless; he felt that one might be able to see into her very essence through them. She was also to be a teacher.

Yeorgos explained that he was referred to as The Commander. However, he explained that the term was not quite suitable as used in the Earth plane. They had not originated on a "free will" planet, and thus, were not plagued by wars, crimes and political nonsense. They had no need of "status" titles, but rather used simple titles representing categoric responsibility. Hypcos was the recognized "medical" person but it was explained that, once again, the definition lacked clarity, for his type of "medical" practice did not resemble anything like that practiced on the human level. Athenia was a technical person who would be classified in Earth language as a scientist/professor. Yeorgos said they all had equivalent skills in most categories but each had his individual area of responsibility. He noted all were skilled pilots to facilitate rotation of flight responsibilities. He promised to demonstrate that skill in a few days.

Athenia interrupted the conversation saying she "felt" energy vibrations, indicating concern regarding the physical person known as Bob. She was correct, as Steve and Diana were deeply concerned about their friend. Athenia said for them to be at ease because Bob had remained in his mortal body and was presently being cared for by their Indian brothers in the Pueblo across the valley. They were told it would be a while before he would be able to see them due to his low vibration density. They would, however, have the ability to observe him. With the training and exercises which were planned for him, however, his would only be a temporary inability. The over all plan was for the three of them to experience the lessons as a group. Athenia continued by sharing that it was planned for the three to function as an integral part of an extremely important mission. The mission was involved with a "GATHERING" and would require extensive explanations. First, she suggested, they should adjust to their new environment.

Yeorgos smiled his captivating smile and said there'd be a lot of fancy footwork and fun which would make the learning period extremely enjoyable. He promised many ship flights for lots of "sight-seeing". He said there were many Earth places of importance that should be pointed out to them. His demeanor reflected the anticipated fun. He pointed out, however, that there would also be many more difficult activities in which to participate, after they returned to the physical form. He figured this should be a most delightful interim. He rambled on about how they would be shown "demonstrations" through pictures using holograms. He then explained that those holograms would consist of active participation within the scenarios. This would be technically produced by a method of displayed projections originating from a laser beam apparatus aboard the craft. He captivated them with his enthusiastic description of how the apparatus functioned; they failed to understand any of it. He said it was the greatest form of entertainment, and they didn't question him regarding that probability. Yeorgos appeared to be completely entertained by everything and had the ability to make the enthusiasm contagious. This new odyssey was undoubtedly going to be remarkable.

After a bit more conversation Yeorgos offered them a tour of the craft which they eagerly accepted.

As they had approached the entry door they all put on insulated foot coverings. It was explained that the insulated footgear would not conduct electricity and would prevent risk of electric shock. The main room appeared to be about twenty-five feet in diameter. Additional rooms were visible off the main room. All light was of some type of indirect arrangement and the room appeared to simply "glow". There was an almost continuous panel of controls surrounding the room, only interrupted by doorways and view tunnels. The "floor" could be made transparent from several locations on the control panel, giving total visibility. In addition, there were multiple view areas for clear visibility above. It appeared the entire ceiling panels could also be converted to a single transparent shield. View ports completely surrounded the craft. Athenia demonstrated many of the technical controls which she pointed out one by one. There were many electromagnetic reactors which were fascinating. Steve's interest was completely absorbed in an antigravity device that was so simple in concept that it baffled his mind; mercury seemed to be the important single element used in the device, although there were also finely tuned copper and gold wires encircling the central "mercury" core. In the energy thrust system there were similar components surrounding what appeared to be a crystal. Yeorgos grinned and assured the two that the devices would be made available to Earthlings when the time was suitable. He also assured them that they would be told of these things during the teaching sessions. Gold was used extensively in the power system and Yeorgos said gold was very easily obtained. Steve chose to let the remark go unquestioned, until a later time.

There was no way Steve and Diana could even begin to imagine the wondrous adventures ahead for them, and in the following days instruction sessions were intense. They saw very little of Richard, Hypcos and John, but Athenia and Yeorgos were with them constantly. They had been given marvelous living quarters and all comforts were provided them. Hours were spent in vibration raising exercises, extensive discussion sessions, as well as intensive input regarding projects under way by the higher energies. Those projects were to be manifested on the Earth plane.

They were continually updated regarding Bob's condition and were assured that he would be ready to join them soon. They were told that the instructions he was receiving from the Indian master were of utmost importance. They would also be given those teachings. Yeorgos said they were very fortunate to be able to experience the Indian guide in such a personal way. He said for the first time the oral teachings of the Ancient Ones would be recorded and made available to Earth people. The Indian Medicine man was currently working on those gifts, after having been given permission by the Ultimate One whom they lovingly referred to as Grandfather. Yeorgos said many wondrous things were being made available to the human brothers and his only wish would be that they would be used wisely. He said time had literally "run out" for further blundering on planet Earth. Either human species would change their "ways" or they would most surely reap destruction. And, because earth activities had now moved out into space in such a way as to endanger safety of the entire universe, participation would now be required from the outer dimensions. He assured them they would have a thorough explanation regarding those subjects.

Yeorgos told them that there were other such groups gathered at other locations throughout the planet, so the emphasis for this group would be on instructions regarding the United States. Other locations would be shown and mentioned only as necessary to complete a project structure and/or when relative to a joint project. He said a very major gathering was being set up currently and that the highest of energy forms from both the spiritual realms and the cosmic realms would be present in the area known as California. Therefore, great emphasis was being placed on the U.S. He explained the necessity of the movie which Bob, Steve and Diana were producing. He said every detail had been a directed project, even if they had not been aware of that, and that each detail had been planned, even to the location. He told them the GATHERING would take place under disguise as a scene in the motion picture. He said the projected filming of the GATHERING would take place in Tehachapi, at the same time that the town would be celebrating its annual Mountain Festival. That way the local people would participate without realizing there was anything, other than the motion picture filming, taking place. He explained why timing had been so important and why it had been necessary to relocate their residence to that place. He promised to discuss the wind energy farms, their use and intended purpose at a later time.

Behind the facade of the movie and the consequent filming, the very HIGHEST ENERGIES would become manifest. In addition, the space brothers would become visible to the humans gathered for film participation. There was planned a great massing of space craft. There would be entity energy exchanges via craft beams. Yeorgos explained that there were already energies working through a human at Edwards Air Force Base near Rosamond to arrange safe passage for the space craft under the guise of "special effects". That would cover the appearance of radar glitches which might be seen from Edwards. The overall plan would be to have the GATHERING, film all the details, have present many of the highest energy forms from spiritual realms, and have human personalities of such prominence, by the dozens, so there would be no misunderstanding as to the validity of the "happening". The space ships as well as galactic commanders and cosmonauts, would also be present in a spectacular display so that no portion of the event would be discredited. Earth astronauts would be brought in under the guise of participation in a peace segment within the movie. Yeorgos emphasized that the astronauts who had experienced space flight were well aware of space craft from other places in the universe. The Hensleys were assured that those necessary for the successful consummation of the project would be properly informed. Preparations were not only under way, but were almost complete.

The days passed quickly and there were several fantastic spacecraft flights. Athenia and Richard had to go to Peru to finalize some arrangements in that location, and Steve and Diana were allowed to accompany them. Richard's and Athenia's plans were to remain in Peru for several days, so schedules were made for Yeorgos to return for them. Yeorgos took a bit of extra time to allow Steve and Diana to see some of the historic land sites. They were shown the Nazca Plains and the giant drawings were explained. They were taken over Machu Pichu and actually into Lake Titicaca. It was totally breathtaking. Yeorgos was spellbinding as a "tour guide" and kept their complete attention with stories and explanations. He told of one known as Thedra who was a very, very special being. She had been sent to Titicaca and while there, was given the greatest of teachings from the Great Master himself. She recorded all the teachings and they were now available through her in Mt. Shasta, California. He said she was now eighty-seven or eighty eight Earth years of age, but was still physically active and remained intellectually brilliant. He said she had become extremely weary of Earth existence and continually told the space brothers who lived with her, and tended her, that she only remained in this dimension to experience the long-awaited "GATHERING". He grinned widely and said he anticipated some dandy happenings at the GATHERING, which would surely "open some Earth eyes, while dropping many Earth chins". He said Thedra was very special within the "space" community also, and her vibrations were so keenly tuned that she already spent much "time" with the brothers on her home planet. He said she would simply "leave" at such time as she was finished here. He commented that Earth man was so blind and narrow of mind not to have perceived these things. He wondered how so many wrong ideas had made their way into Earth society. He allowed as how he was here to change some of those misconceptions and it would happen very soon!

Before returning to Utah they were given a grand tour. Yeorgos pointed out dozens of sites where there were hidden space bases.

They were also shown the ancient ruins of the Incas, Aztecs and Mayans. Special emphasis was placed on the little country of Belize and the ancient ruins located there. It was there that one of the famed "crystal skulls" was found; Yeorgos explained the secret of the skulls, and the importance of their locations. They talked of important locations within the United States, but a decision was made to investigate those when Bob would be with them, due to planned personal involvement for the three Earth beings. The time was growing near for Bob to be joining them, Yeorgos said.

GLORIOUS LIFE

When Bob awakened it was dark and he was thirsty, but still too weak to make any effort to move. He made a mental note to himself that he felt no pain and was thankful. He was too weak and confused to even think about it; it was as if he had been drugged. He felt a great peace and drifted back into sleep. This time he was aware it was sleep, and not a loss of consciousness. He didn't know where he was, he assumed he was still on the river bank, he didn't care one way or another. The next time he came to, it was broad daylight but the sun had not yet risen. He could hear water running--it sounded wonderful. Before he could make any effort at movement an arm was slipped under his head and an earthen vessel of water (he could smell the clay and feel the roughness with his lips) was held to his mouth. He drank thirstily and lay back. He could see the sun would shine into the area where he lay after rising a little higher, and he was glad. In spite of the fact he was covered with a sort of furry blanket, he was chilled and the warmth of the sun would be welcome indeed. His own clothing had been removed and his arm was straightened and splinted with a pack of some kind of fragrant herb on the open wound which the jagged bone had made in his arm. He also noted that his right knee and left ankle and foot were also wrapped in herbal bandages. He had learned this by careful probing, then settled back and relaxed. He felt no pain and realized he was being cared for, and he sure needed it!

The first day or two drifted by hazily as Bob fought illness, strangeness and lassitude. He became aware that an Indian woman was sitting across the center of the room from him. She was holding a small loom on her lap on which she wove threads from big balls of coarse string of what looked like a kind of cotton or wool. Sometimes she wove rabbit fur cut into strips into a blanket like the one that covered him. Back at the far end of the long room, which was more like an adobe cave than a building, sat an old Medicine Man making arrowheads, or something similar. There was a pile of flint behind him and it appeared he was fashioning the points and tools from pieces taken from it. Bob could hear the tap, tap, chip, chip of his craft all day. Often, one or both of these people helped care for him.

He had not yet really seen the person who was mostly caring for him, because she (he knew it was a woman because of her light, exquisite scent) seemed to be always back of him, or above his head. On the third afternoon however, he saw her move over to where a spring ran water near the opening of the room. The water cascaded gently over the stone catch basin and splashed happily over the small stones at the base of the basin. She had gone to get fresh water for him. She was returning, carrying a small bowl, when he looked up. He has always thought the Indian girls were pretty, but never had he seen anyone to equal this girl. She was so beautiful he couldn't believe his eyes and thought to himself that perhaps he had perished after all. She brought the bowl to him, gave him a drink, bathed his face and gently smiled at him. She then turned toward the room opening and settled on the sand shelf at the foot of his pallet. He studied her as she began working on pieces of leather which were obviously intended to be shoes. The leather was soft as butter and appeared to be from the same material as the clothing which had been placed on his body. He wondered what her name might be. He watched a while and studied her eyes as they were like the wide, bottomless eyes of a doe and decided he would call her Fawn; she reminded him of a graceful and gentle Fawn. Every time he looked at her he felt an unbelievable tug at his heart because, if he had not known better, he would have been sure she was Anaranjia. The memories caused bittersweet pain as he marveled at the similarities of this girl and his lost love from Peru.

From his pallet he could look out and see across the valley, a large bit of sky and a bit of what appeared to be a cliff ledge jutting out in front of the room opening.

Fawn was always the one who brought food, fed him from an earthen bowl, and wiped his hands and face with a damp, coarse cloth. Every evening she brought him a bowl of some kind of herbal tea, kind of faintly bitter but decidedly sweet and aromatic. After he drank it, he always slipped into a deep sleep that would last all night. His arm was mostly comfortable and he had the feeling it was healing rapidly. The swelling in his legs was greatly reduced although he had not tried to bear weight on them. He was still too weak to make the effort to even sit. After a few more days Fawn stopped bringing the evening bowl of tea and Bob was awake more during the night. No one remained in his room at night; he was alone with his thoughts and dreams.

In the early mornings, the Medicine Man stood at the mouth of the cave and chanted his greeting to the sun. On his way back to the flint bed he always stopped and put his hands on Bob's injuries, one at a time, and Bob could feel the heat go deep into the injured tissues. Apparently, this had been going on every morning before he woke, but now that he was stronger, he was more aware of what was happening around him.

He noticed that a group of workers filed out of the kiva in the north end of the cave-like room and, from the simple tools they carried, he deduced they were farmers raising crops in the valley, probably using water from the spring for irrigation. In the afternoon a few children, ten or a dozen, came out and were tended by a couple of older girls. There might have been a pool below where the spring ran off because he could hear the children splashing around in water. Later in the afternoon, the children all filed back past him and he couldn't tell exactly where they went.

Bob knew very little of Indian customs other than from stories told by an old Indian who helped at the Roost Ranch. He had enjoyed the fascinating stories told by the old man and eagerly looked forward to the evenings spent at the ranch with Steve.

One of the legends was that the Indians had come up through the sipapu in the bottom of the kiva to inhabit the Earth. He had seen the sipapus in the floors of kivas, rectangles about eighteen inches long and four inches or so wide, carved a few inches into the floor of the kiva. These indentations were always kept meticulously clean and the Indians said they often communicated with the Spirit World through them. Bob wondered if it could possibly be that this clan was just emerging to raise crops and store food in the caves below for their final emergence the next spring. This large cave-like room in which he now lived was obviously ceremonial for the Indians treated it as Holy Ground, hardly ever disturbing a grain of sand. Was it possible that the clan might be returning to the Spirit World through the sipapu every night? "Oh boy," he thought, "is my mind on a wild kick now."

As the days slipped by into what Bob thought must be weeks, he realized he was captivated by Fawn. One day as she sat nearby, he became overcome with her beauty and grace and reached out to pull her roughly into his arms. He grasped her arm, and the Weaver stood up; he caught a movement from the Medicine Man. A wave of fear washed over him; he instinctively knew that his action would not be tolerated, that he must treat Fawn with careful consideration. Well, that suited him well enough, for by now he was deeply in love with her.

The following day as she again sat nearby, he burst out: "I only wish you could talk to me !"

"I can talk to you," she looked at him in surprise.

"Well, why haven't you, then?" And as he was struck with a new thought, "And in my language, too!"

She laughed, a tinkling brook-water sound, and answered: "You didn't ask me before. And we are not actually talking any language, just from one mind to the other, really. You have to open your mind to another person to talk to him."

Bob begged how to make his approach, and Fawn said that first must come desire--nothing was ever possible without desire first. When one desired deeply enough, he could open his mind to another, and if that other wanted to communicate, both minds were open and tuned to each other.

Bob was not entirely convinced. He pointed to the shouting children. Again, her tinkle of amusement and she said, "They are not actually talking as such, although we do have words and our chants are words. But mostly they are just making sounds somewhat like the singing of birds."

He listened a moment and she was right, they did sound a bit like birds!

One afternoon after Fawn had left him, Bob got up and moved over to the Weaver and sat down near her. If desire was the key he had plenty of that; he desperately needed to find out what was going on.

It required many sessions and endless attempts but finally, he learned that this was a group set up to come out through the sipapu and inhabit the Earth, as he had fantasized. "This is too incredible!" he thought to himself. He was told that this was what they called the linking year, when they were raising and storing crops to last them until they could get settled. They had built many dwellings and several villages. They were building storage holes and also storing in caves along the ledges north of this one, which they did use for ceremonial purposes. He learned also, that Fawn was the beloved daughter of the Supreme Spirit and, only because of that, she was allowed to be of the world for just this summer. When Bob asked if she was coming out with the clan, the Weaver assured him that she was not, her father would probably never let her leave the Spirit World. Then the Weaver closed her mind, communication stopped, and Bob had to be content with the bit he had learned.

Bob was certainly not content with the prospects of losing yet another love. If Fawn could not come out, then how was he going to arrange to get to go through the sipapu and be with her? It took a day or two for him to get the Weaver to talk to him again, she seemed to be afraid to say very much but at last he asked her point blank if there was any way he could go back through the sipapu. She was stark silent for a moment and he thought he had angered her, "Damn, why had he been so blunt?"

"With Faith, anything is possible," she finally whispered.

"Anything is possible?" Bob was fascinated with this new idea.

"But only with faith." The Weaver paused in her work to give him her undivided attention; something she had not done before, and he was almost sorry she was now, from the severe look on her face. "Only with faith! Talk to the Medicine Man." Her mind snapped shut, ending the discussion, and Bob had to go back to his pallet to think this over.

Bob was in total awe of the Medicine Man. He knew how the Indians revered these leaders. He felt he couldn't simply go up and start asking a bunch of questions. If he could just take some gift--and his mind searched for something. He had not had need of the clothing which the Indians had removed when he was brought here, and he spotted them cleanly washed and folded on a little shelf on the far wall. He hobbled over to them and, surely enough, the things he had been carrying in his pockets were all there. He inventoried the contents and decided upon using his pocket knife.

When he worked up his courage, he approached the Medicine Man and knelt down as he had watched the children that the Medicine Man coached, do. The old seer looked up, smiled, and opened his mind to Bob, and Bob said he had a gift for him. He took out the knife and opened it. He was glad he always kept the edge honed razor sharp. He pulled a hair from his head and snipped it off an inch or so from where he held it in his fingers.

The Medicine Man reached back of him, struck off a chip of flint, and, taking a hair from his own head he indicated that Bob should hold one end. Then he delicately and carefully split the hair. Bob watched the little curls of spider-web fineness curl up and suddenly he knew the truth--they didn't need any of his so-called technology. Their culture was not physical, it was more refined than Bob's and their stone tools were certainly adequate. The meeting was congenial, however, and Bob offered the knife anyway. The seer smiled, nodded his acceptance and thanked him for the gift with gracious poise. Bob became aware that his own perception had been considerably sharpened by this experience.

After a bit, Bob looked at the old wise one again. He had to know and this was the only way he could find out. As carefully as he could, he asked if it would be possible for a mortal to go back through the sipapu, saying that he loved Fawn with all his heart and he wanted to go and be with her for all time and eternity.

The old man chipped silently at a magnificent arrowhead for a time and Bob was afraid he going to be told nothing. Then after chip, chip, chip for a few minutes, the old man held out the arrowhead for Bob to inspect. Then he took it back, laid it carefully on a second flint and with one chip broke it into two pieces. The old man smiled wisely and said there were ways to do everything if one had the desire and patience to learn. He handed the two pieces of flint to Bob to make his point.

After a time the old man said that this matter had already come up in the Councils and they were aware that Fawn and Bob were in love. It depended on Bob, if he wanted to learn the rituals and chants and then go through the spiritual teachings for purification, perhaps he could go through the sipapu with Fawn. Only after he had properly prepared himself, could he try. He would be allowed to begin learning the next day if that was his desire. Bob's heart sang and as he hobbled to the doorway, he let out a bellowing yell to the redtail hawk circling above.

For days upon days, Bob studied and worked as he had never studied before in his life. He spent hours every day at the feet of the Medicine Man, repeating the chants, correcting his speech, going over and over difficult phrases. The old mystic sometimes laid aside his work and led Bob in a chant, almost as if he were a music master, but often he just went on with his own work. The old man would lapse into hours of uninterrupted teaching of old handed down legends. Bob had grown to love this being with reverence and respect. They laughed a lot too, as the wise old man was filled with humor which he shared liberally. Bob was told there were many surprises in store for him while he dwelled here within the canyons, to not be closed to anything that might occur. He was assured that he would receive the inner sight to accept those things and not to allow doubts and shock to preclude his receiving the guidance. He was told that he would be allowed to experience a great happening that had been setup eons before. He was also told that great knowledge would be opened up and truths presented which could not be disclaimed by the masses of human entities, that the time had drawn nigh for a gathering of the highest universal energies. Bob wanted to pursue the subject, but the old man had turned off and he knew no more discussion would take place that day.

As the lessons drew to a close, the old seer placed a calm hand on his shoulder and said, "Remember, my son, with faith anything is possible".

It was fairly late in the afternoon and Fawn would be coming soon. Bob was restless, and wanted to tell her that he would be leaving the next morning to go into the mountains to meditate and pray and make himself eligible to pass with her through the sipapu. When she appeared, she was radiant with happiness; she already knew,

They sat quietly together for a while. They didn't talk much; words were not necessary to share this togetherness. Then, Bob remembered the broken arrowhead. He pulled the pieces out and they looked at them. Bob took the larger piece and tucked it into a pocket of the shirt he was wearing. He extended his other hand and offered the pointed piece to Fawn. He told her to keep it always for, as with themselves, when the pieces were placed together, they formed a unit--a whole. He smiled and said that each time she looked at her portion, she would think of him and they would always be together that way.

PLATE V

THE RAINBOW BALLET

One day following his lessons, which had been of such strong spiritual nature that he was weary from thinking on them, he was restless and it was too early for Fawn to come back to him, so he paced the area nervously. He fidgeted for awhile then did something he had never done before, went in search of Fawn. His legs had healed and his walks had become quite long, and he really enjoyed the time spent in the out of doors. His arm was almost healed and he was able to use it without discomfort for some tasks; actually, he felt extremely well. As he strolled along the valley floor, he noticed a side canyon which had not come to his attention before. He usually walked with Fawn so decided he likely had been too involved with her to have noticed it. It was a short canyon and at the head of the valley was a particularly beautiful alcove, the cliffs sheltering and rounding behind a fin of rock jutting out from the canyon wall into which the ages had carved a sandstone arch. The front of the arch rested on a high rock buttress, a butte that was crowned from the level of the arch top by a thin, cone-like spire that reached several feet into the air. At the foot of the butte, under the arch, the floods had left a level plain of some yards in diameter which looked like a stage. There had also been some spectacular Indian drawings scattered all along the cliff walls as he passed along the trail.

Suddenly, he was stopped in stunned disbelief. From behind the arch, a gossamer clad maiden appeared and vaulted to the top of the arch, trailing a segment of living rainbow several yards in length. She flung the gauzy membrane into the air and it furled and floated above her as if immune to gravity. The scene in itself was enough to boggle his mind but, still staring with unblinking eyes, he collapsed on a small ledge jutting out beside him; he was staring into the eyes of Diana. Before he could think, a second maiden sprang out to meet Diana; she too carried a swirling rainbow section. The second dancer was Fawn and Bob went dumb. "What can be happening?" his mind screamed. Diana and Fawn were then joined by five other maidens which could have only been spirit forms, it appeared to Bob. Each had a rainbow section, and the air of the alcove seemed to shimmer and radiate with veils of vibrant color. Muted music guided and timed the swirling and twirling dance of the spirit maidens. Following Diana, the company made a circle around the top of the alcove, the rainbows floating, furling, coiling in the space above the alcove. The music picked up a beat, as the dancers again landed on the arch, and the music changed into a triumphal march, dominated by stringed instruments of some sort. The dancers suddenly drew in the gossamer streamers and reissued them in gigantic flashing pom-poms. Every frond of every pom-pom flickered and flashed as the girls gyrated, pirouetted, turned handsprings and swung back and forth on the arch tip in a frenzy of controlled maneuvers, the pom-poms sweeping up, around and below the arch until there was an effect of pulsing radiance shooting out in every direction like the bursting of multicolored fireworks in the sky. In a final exuberant gesture, the spirit dancers cast the pom-poms high into the air and drew them back, changed once again into the rainbow streamers. Diana was the central dancer and it appeared as if this might be some sort of ritual lesson; more shared than taught.

Down again onto the floor of the alcove they tumbled, drawing in the rainbows. Then in a whirling pirouette, they cast them up where they flared like a cloud of smoke, the free and flickering ends licking like flames from a multicolored fire.

The alcove seemed to darken until Bob had the feeling it was night. As the dancers whirled in the alcove, they were suddenly joined by two men from either side of the arch. The men were dressed in tight-fitted costumes which mostly resembled those of ballet dancers, but the music was definitely what he considered Indian rhythm. Diana and the two men proceeded to perform a most spectacular dance and after a few minutes, Fawn joined the three. Bob did not recognize the male dancers and this was a great relief to him; he had experienced about all he could handle. He continued to stare in amazement as the remaining spirit maidens rejoined those on the stage and five additional male dancers joined the fray. The girls drew their streamers into scarfs and filled the canyon with flashes of flickering light far more intense than lightning, even if only brief flashes. The music diminished somewhat and then burst forth with more intensity than ever as that portion of the dance wound down to a swirling finish of fluorescence in spectacularly dazzling display of radiance; the light in the canyon seemed to be restored without his noticing at what point it had returned.

The dancers flung up the sections of rainbow into the sky. As the music changed and fell into the sensuous beat of a hauntingly beautiful waltz, they manipulated the diaphanous cloud into golden lilies, taller than themselves, and Bob noted their costumes had changed and were now iridescent silver-white with golden trimmings. The golden lilies didn't seem to really touch the floor, but they bent, swayed and twirled, lifting and swinging the beautiful dancers whose graceful movements swayed and flashed to the beat of the music. The metallic lilies seemed to somehow support, to enfold, to lift and display them. Then he realized the lilies were actually the men and the levitation an illusion. The couples moved in complicated figures and Diana always seemed to be the "star" of the show. Bob thought even the stars in the sky must sway to this beauty and know that these dancers belonged above with them.

As the music and waltz reached a climax, Diana spun from the formation and snapped the golden lily again into a gauzy segment of color. Leaping to the top of the arch, towing her rainbow, she suddenly dived through the arch, up and over it again, and perched on the tip of the spire. She now appeared to be a violet iris flower within the rainbow, her lovely face peeping out from the upturned petals above the fall-petal in front. As she perched atop the spire, the whole alcove seemed to fill with a soft, suspended mist. The fragrance came to Bob and the freshness seemed literally to touch his skin. Suddenly, the aroma seemed like that of the potion he had received his first few nights in the village and he was completely lost in the smell of the dance.

Diana flicked out her rainbow fragment, almost invisible in the glory of the mist as Fawn, a pink iris, came up through the arch, leaving it swathed in a changing rosy glow and, wheeling in close to Diana, the colors merged and seemed to fill the stage. This was all so sudden that Bob was not surprised to see the purples run up the rainbow on the edge as the pink came down the side like they were being painted on by gigantic watercolor brush strokes. The music changed again, this time to vibrant, haunting drums. One by one the other dancers entered the archway, each having the appearance of a varicolored flower with their matching streamers floating about them. The stage was splashed with color and, as the men rejoined the dancers, Bob was held spellbound by the rhythm and coordination of their movements. The dance was spectacular as the drums reached a thunderous reverberation that seemed to control the dance and all the Earth around it. The dancers raised their rainbow streamers which seemed to merge into one, stretching away to the farther canyon rim. The drumbeat then changed once more and it was as if Bob caught a warning, a feeling of disaster in the thunder, a foretelling of doom. Diana and Fawn were somehow changed into yellow spider-web wrapped forms. Towing their rainbows into position, they turned apart and perched on the farther canyon rims opposite each other. The other dancers sank still circling, and the sweet aroma and moistness of the air sank with them.

As Bob watched Diana and Fawn spread their arms and, holding the rainbow in their fingertips, pulled it taught, flipped it a couple of times, and flung it into the sky. The drums screamed in protest. The rainbow arched up and like a ripple in a pool, disappeared as the drums stopped mid-beat--silence was absolutee--movement ceased--only the hawk circling above continued its endless glide across the silence of the heavens. Bob sat in wonder, oblivious of everything around him; he failed to even notice the arm which was placed across his shoulders from behind. His being still throbbed to the beat of the drums, his mind filled with flashes of half-formed ideas which tumbled in an incoherent kaleidoscope. Gradually, his body quieted and his mind began to find its focus again.

Now he could comprehend the message the Medicine Man had given him--that he must purify himself, purge himself of his mortality and become pure spirit to be able to move into the beyond through the sipapu. To obtain that excellence, he realized he must undergo a metamorphosis as complete as a chrysalis produces a butterfly from the larvae.

Death was one answer, but there had to be an alternative. To believe that was the only way was over-simplification. He had watched as Diana died in the river and yet here she was. How could it be that she was here? His earthly being was overcome and yet he knew he had moved into a higher spiritual existence. He would gladly die for Fawn, but that didn't seem to be the solution. The Medicine Man had told him that anything was possible with faith, but he knew his faith didn't include letting control of his circumstances completely out of his own hands. Death was surely more of an ending than a beginning in his book. He had always considered life after death a total whistling in the dark to relieve the streaks of fear of the inevitable. Another thing that had always lived in his belief was that one died when his time came and not before, and never was it acceptable to die by any controlled method.

He was convinced by his experience with the after-effects of watching the dance that unless he divested himself of this earthly humanness, his mortality, he could never attain the level of Fawn, even if he did go through the sipapu with her. He carefully reviewed what the Medicine Man had told him. It seemed that there was a slim chance that he could purify himself with meditation and prayer; and he was as ready as he ever would be to give it a try. He turned to look for Fawn to tell her that tomorrow he would go alone into the mountains and make himself worthy of her. But she was not there. Instead, he looked directly into the eyes of Steve.

SMALL REVELATIONS

It was a joyous time. After the initial shock of finding Steve and Diana, Bob ceased the incessant questioning of "how" it could be this way and accepted that it was. When he realized Athenia and Richard were also in the group, he was totally happy. Fawn never said that she had once been Anaranjia and Bob didn't pry; everything seemed wonderful to him.

Yeorgos said the teaching sessions would be speeded up and that many would be joining them for many of the teachings. He said that many Earth beings joined the groups during what Earthlings called sleep. These would be the beings who would be working on the Earth plane.

Yeorgos had received a message from Athenia that she and Richard had concluded their work in Peru sooner than anticipated, and had requested that they be "gathered" and returned to the canyon so that they might also attend the lessons. Diana, Steve and Bob were all included in the flight to Peru. Yeorgos made sure Bob had a chance to briefly see most of the things Diana and Steve had already experienced, simply for the fun of the experience. Then, after picking up Richard and Athenia, they were given another very special tour.

They were taken over many sites that were considered "sacred" as well as being shown places historically connected with space sightings in the U.S. The locations ranged all over the U.S.; the Devils Rock in Wyoming, Monument Valley and several other places in Arizona, several places in Texas and an Indian area in Oklahoma, two special places in the Smokey Mountains and Appalachian chain, and on and on it seemed to Bob. There apparently were hundreds of places with special bases or ports; many ceremonial places where great meetings were continually taking place. It was a fantastic experience.

Then Yeorgos took time to do something very special for the Earthlings. He took them to places where there were things of personal interest. He informed them in advance that many things would be explained at a later time in an overall view of priority projects, but they were to be shown where they personally fit into the tapestry.

He laughed and said that many times while plans were being made on a conscious level relating to the overall plan, messages were sent through channels not understood by the Earthlings. He reminded Diana of receiving warnings and advice from as far away as Chicago and New Jersey, through people she did not know. Now, they would be given an opportunity to make some of those connections so they might better understand what was planned on the higher levels.

First they covered the area of Mt. Shasta and looked, in detail, at an area on the Pit River called Big Bend Hot Springs. This was the area Bob, Steve and Diana planned to install geothermal power production units as well as research a food supplement algae. Yeorgos said it was the proper project but that the turbines should be set on the highest ridges near the river bend because there would be failure of hydroelectric installations further up the river, causing the entire river bed area to be devastated by waters from the dams. He continued by saying it would be alright to use the area for a brief time for some greenhouse research, but to not plan to place the major greenhouse project on that property. He suggested that there would be sufficient room in the Tehachapi area, as was now planned, to facilitate those greenhouses. He said there would be other food products that would be given later to be used in times of emergency. He also said that synchronous generators must be used in the turbines to facilitate direct usage of the electricity.

Next, they went to the Tehachapi area and looked over the mountain areas and all the electric production wind farms. He said the turbines Steve planned to construct would far surpass the capabilities of any currently being utilized. These would be the Westinghouse 600 kilowatt model. He said that because of synchronous generators, the power could be instantly utilized without the necessity of the utility distribution should that system fail. He said that wind power could help fill in temporarily should the other systems be closed down for emergency reasons. He also said they would be given information regarding a device invented by Nikola Tesla which would attach to the base of the turbine tower and would produce mammoth amounts of energy utilizing vibrations from the tower itself. It would be a very simple device using highly tuned wires and quick silver (mercury). He continued that as man would grow spiritually to a level where he no longer threatened his own universe, the method of universal power production would be given the group. It, too, would be a simple device originally discovered by Nikola Tesla. It would function on rays from the sun and copper sheets (in addition to highly tuned wires). It would not however, require direct sunlight so could function at times when the atmosphere was clouded for any reason. He added that the electricity distribution system would not require wires, but would rather be "beamed" from tall towers and then distributed to individual "receiving" devices. He concluded by saying there would be many instructions given this group as there was much to be done if man would survive his own destructive nature. He said that the underground nuclear explosions detonated in February of 1987 had been the "straw that broke the camel's back". The reaction had set into motion vibrations of such magnitude (added to those already being experienced at that time) that the result could not be reversed by outside forces. There would be massive earthquakes triggered as those vibration waves spread out and impacted the Earth fault lines.

He said what would result would be some massive earthquakes which would effectively cut off the coastal areas. Power lines would fall, water supply conduits would be broken and fuel lines would be severed; these would be the very most minimal damages. Further, the road systems would be unusable and the massive irrigation system of the agriculture areas would be devastated, thus causing food shortages of tremendous proportions.

PLATE VI

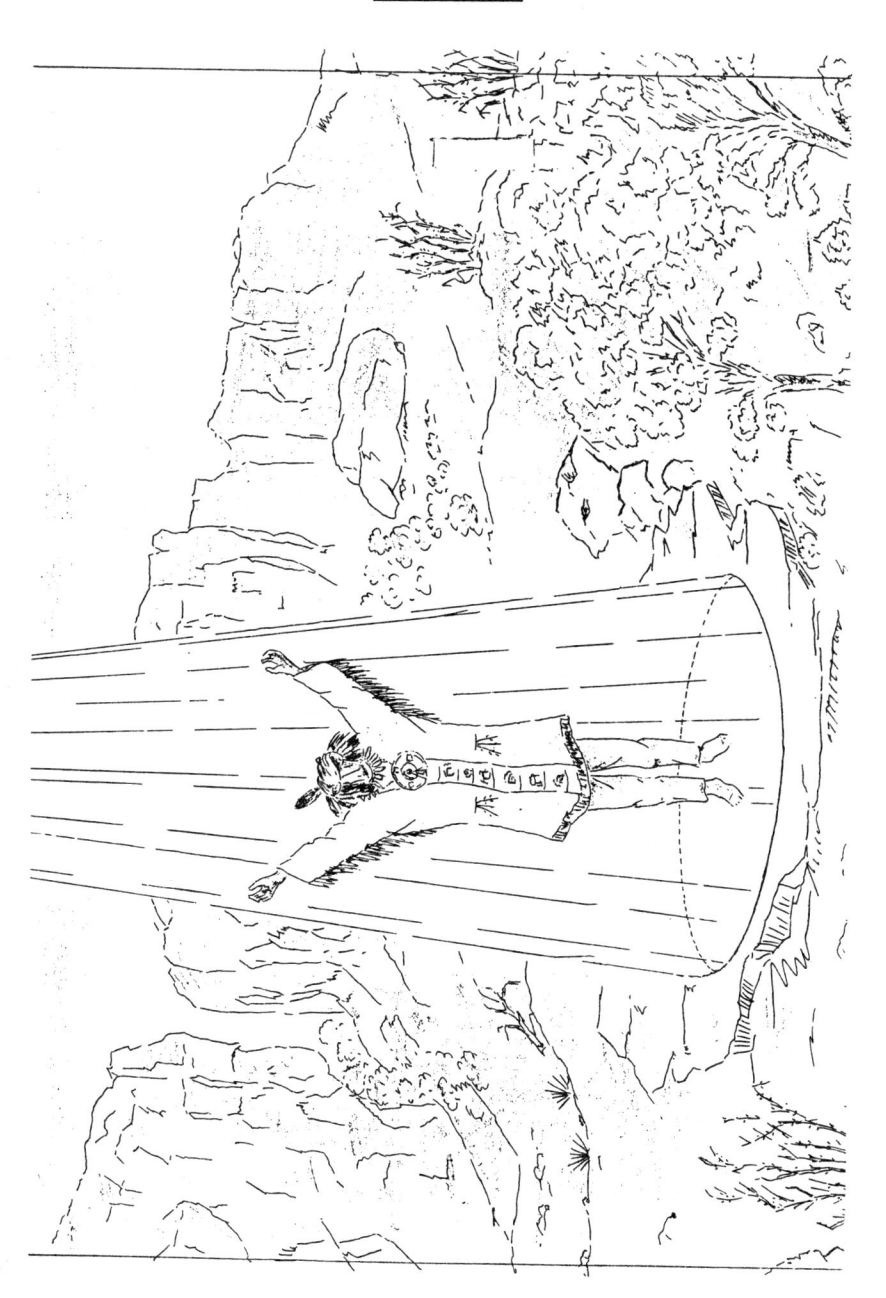

ANCIENT REVELATIONS

It was evening when the groups began to gather up the canyon for holograms and speakers. As Steve and the Earth group joined the audience they noted many people whom they had not seen before. The gathering was situated in a widened area and those in attendance sat clustered facing a sheer cliff wall with an outcropping of rock at its base. As the natural light faded, it was replaced by a "spot-light" from the space craft which lit the "stage" area. It was wonderful as the sky was visible above the stream of light. They could watch the stars take their places in the universe while waiting for the session to begin.

Spotted Eagle climbed to a point near the middle of the rock outcropping and raised his hands to the Heavens. There was the scent of smoke wafting on the air and Spotted Eagle carried some feathered items, in addition to a beautifully decorated, long-stemmed pipe. The audience fell into immediate silence as he took his place and prepared to speak.

Spotted Eagle spoke of the Ancient Ones and of the relationships of every creation on Earth, of the relationship of humans to all of those creations. He spoke of the beauty and harmony of Earth as our mother, and as he spoke the cliff became a huge "screen" upon which was projected a collage of action pictures. He continued to narrate as scene after scene was illuminated before the group.

The projections showed the devastation perpetrated by man on the two beautiful continents known as the Americas. Among those things shown were consequences of acid rain with dozens of examples of streams, rivers, large and small lakes, and oceans being polluted and destroyed; there were pictures of forests being poisoned by pollution, devastated by man for industry and cleared for agriculture. The consequential terrible flooding from the stripped watersheds was shown. He showed pictures of dozens of electric power plants, oil refineries, chemical and industrial plants belching forth pollution. He showed the destruction resulting from mining activities (there were also demonstrations of Earth collapse into some of the underground mine shafts as the Earth shifted). The examples seemed endless.

Spotted Eagle even showed examples of man's desecration of Earth's most sacred areas; the human faces carved onto the face of magnificent Black Hills (one of the Indian's most sacred spiritual places). Diana was openly sobbing and Bob could not stop the flow of tears from his eyes. Somehow he knew the subject matter would not get easier as the evening progressed. He would be correct in that assumption.

FUTURE REVELATIONS

John, too, was accompanied by projected visual holograms which made an individual have the feeling of actual participation within the scene itself. As he spoke, appropriate visualizations moved with his verbal illusions.

He said he would simply be giving a description of things as directly handed down to him, without personal comment. He then launched into his teachings:

"And it is said there shall be winds, and there shall be, in the time when it is winter; and the trees shall bow down their boughs, and the winds shall sting with the cold; and there shall be great suffering among the people and they shall fall down and cry for mercy.

"And there shall be a mighty earthquake and it shall split in twain the country of North America, and it shall be as nothing the world has known before, for it shall be that there shall be a great part of the great land of the north continent go down and a great sea shall form within her center part from the Dominion of Canada into the Gulf of Mexico.

"And there shall be great ocean liners, liners which shall travel within its waters which will be propelled by solar energy of the next age. But with this, they shall be unable to travel east to west or from west to east, through what is now the Atlantic Ocean for it shall have a mountain range which has been thrown up from the bottom of the Atlantic; and it shall be extended into the air to the altitude of ten thousand feet and it shall be the City of old, for it was the Light of the world. She went down amid a great shock and a great wave; and it shall be that she shall come up the same way as she went down.

"And the west side shall be as the sheer side of granite, and it shall be without foothold; and the way shall be as the eagle flies from the place which is Upper Virginia three hundred miles due east; and at this point it shall be one thousand and eight hundred feet from the waters; and not an entrance through the land shall there be to the east, for it is not for them which are to be the remnants, to communicate by water; for it shall be with a new science, and a new method shall be given unto them. For there is not a place which is that shall remain the same in its present state.

"And not a person shall be left which is not prepared for that which shall be. And there are many called but few are chosen: for there are none which have been chosen which have not been carefully prepared; and they have been unto themselves true, and they have given credit where credit is due. And now it is given unto them to be the seed of the new Civilization which shall come upon the Earth.

"And within the time which is left before this shall come upon the Earth, it shall be that many will be called: and they shall doubt; and they shall fear; and they shall faint; and they shall fall by the way; and they shall be in no wise, for it is given unto man to fear that which he does not understand--and for that does he wait.

"And it is said there shall be winds, and there shall be the winds, and they shall be as none the Earth has known; and they shall be as the winds from the sea and from the land all rolled into one great tempest. And they shall be as the winds of the North and the South and East and the West, and they shall tear that which is in their path and they shall be as the reaper who mows down that which is in his path. And they shall sing with the bitterness of the cold. And they shall be as the elements of the Earth, for they shall contain both rain and wind; and the hail shall be as big as bird eggs, and it shall split that which it hits.

"And it shall be that the suffering shall be great upon the Earth, for it is given unto man to know suffering. And he has not known such suffering before, and when it is come upon him, he shall fall down and shall cry for mercy.

"And it shall be that the winds too shall be great upon the Earth--they shall blow east, west, north and south and not a place shall there be upon the Earth which shall escape the winds which bloweth; and when this tribulation has come upon the Earth, it shall be that there shall be many who have kept within the law.

"And with the coming of the winds and belching of fire from within the Earth there shall be--MORE!"

John continued by telling of how things would be. He said that no one would be responsible for the words of another nor would any man take upon himself that which would be done by another. Each entity would be responsible for his own. He said man had lost his identity with the Father God which had sent him and that if he would not awaken and return to the Father he would surely perish.

John spoke on for a very long time giving illustration after illustration. He concluded by saying it was time to talk more about the present.

PLATE VII

PRESENT REVELATIONS

John explained that there were many Space Brothers here to assist us through the transition and time of tribulation; they could help us, but they could do no more. They would be allowed to help only as requested by Earthlings with one exception and this was stressed emphatically: "YOU MAY NOT TAKE YOUR WEAPONS OF DESTRUCTION INTO SPACE. BEYOND TWO-HUNDRED-FIFTY MILES BEYOND YOUR SURFACE, YOU WILL BE STOPPED! NEITHER WILL YOU BE ALLOWED TO CREATE THE ULTIMATE NUCLEAR DESTRUCTION OF THE TOTALITY OF THE PLANET ITSELF; THE IMPACT TO THE UNIVERSE WOULD BE TOO DEVASTATING AND THE BROTHERS WOULD BE GIVEN PERMISSION TO PREVENT SUCH AN OCCURRENCE." He then turned and invited Yeorgos to take the platform. He said Yeorgos would present the teachings from the aspect of Space Brothers and the Interplanetary Councils.

Yeorgos was also accompanied by the picture projections as were appropriate to emphasize points.

He said the brothers were prepared to work closely with Earthlings at such time as they were accepted and asked to participate. He said their technology is of such magnitude that Earth man would be unable to comprehend the power. He was assuring Earthlings, however, that even though they could destroy us or make slaves of us, etc., they came in love and co-existence within the Cosmos. They would not presume to do anything other than as requested with the one exception as told by John.

He emphasized that during the upcoming period, until Earth moves into her new cycle, she would be belching forth increased disturbances upon her surface. As plates shift beneath the oceans' floors there would be increased tidal wave activity. The resulting shifts would bring about disturbances of those thought of as "sleeping" volcanos. Those would begin to rumble and spew forth molten lava that would come quickly and with minimal warning. This would increase as the climactic conditions were altered. There would be increased swelling of streams.

Riverbeds would enlarge and they would not recede to their pre-existent condition. There would be peninsulas and small isthmuses that were going to vanish most abruptly and quickly.

The geophysical face of the Earth would begin its alteration during this period. Those areas where oceans' waters have crept in most gradually and quietly would be accelerated, and indeed, sleeping valleys would be filled overnight. And man on Earth would look about and wonder what is happening.

Yeorgos continued: "Because of the decrease in the ozone layer about Earth there is an increased heat that is coming from the Central Sun. This is bringing about resultant melting of your polar caps, again with resultant climactic changes.

"Man of Earth shall quickly come to recognize that Earth is revolting against the treatment that she has received. This shall be a warning, a preview of what is in store for man if he does not immediately alter his ways.

"At this time the vibratory pattern of Earth itself is such that no alteration of her course is anticipated; she has been released from her role as a buffer, and she now BEGINS HER OWN CLEANSING! Man will now be accountable for his own cleansing.

"Earth is entering a phase of two seasons: summer and winter, with extreme temperatures in each. Fall and Spring will cease to be recognized. Man should lay up stores and provisions for seasons shall not be as kind to Earth as man has known in the past. Man's time of great bounty and food abundance will greatly be altered. Space brothers stand ready, however, to render help and instructions in that area. Food substances which will suffice for survival will be given to appropriate ones on the planet, and properly prepared, will be quite palatable.

"Man must learn to share freely in order to survive. There will be great shortages in food supplies and also proclaimed shortages in your fossil fuels as they are hoarded and usurped for reasons of greed. You will find yourselves without transportation because there will be no fuel to run your machinery. You will need the substitute foods to feed yourselves.

"There will be great energy shortages, electricity will become unavailable for many reasons, therefore, you must learn to minimize your needs. You must begin to rely on those elemental winds and patterns that will bring you those energies that you need. You must make your dwelling places strong, sturdy and well insulated so that they will serve you well. We will show you methods of using compressed earth which will replace wood and other things as primary structural material.

"We are prepared to teach you methods of health care which will allow you to remain active and energized during this period of time. There will be widespread death from diseases which are currently incurable by your present medical methods.

"You must expect gigantic changes within your government structures as your present monetary systems become chaotic. There will be no money for taxes and without taxes there will be a rapid withdrawal of politicians and the chain of events will cause the governmental structure, as it now operates, to fail. There must be those available to fill the void and rebuild with a new and different type of system which brings harmony to the peoples of all Earth nations."

Yeorgos continued for a long period of time along the same lines of subject matter and then began to make his concluding remarks. He said he wanted to frighten no one and certainly all panic must be avoided. He said he would, however, speak of the ultimate evacuation process, should that become a necessity. He spoke: "We have come to fulfill the destiny of this planet, which is to experience a short period of 'cleansing' and then to usher in a new and golden age of Light. I will henceforth refer to that period as the time of Radiance.

"As mentioned before, the souls of Light are you people of Earth who have lived according to universal truths and who recognize GOD as the SOURCE OF ALL THAT IS GOOD; THE SOURCE OF 'ALL THINGS'. The short period of cleansing is

IMMINENT--EVEN THE MIDNIGHT HOUR! But, we have been informed of this and have made preparations for that event. I will explain how it will be so that it will relieve any anxieties amongst those present.

"We of space have millions of space ships stationed in the skies above your planet ready to instantly lift you off at the first warning of your planet's beginning to tilt on its axis. When this happens, we have only a VERY SHORT PERIOD OF TIME in which to lift you from the surface before great tidal waves will lash your coastline--possibly five miles or more high! They will cover much of your land masses!

"These tidal waves will unleash great earthquakes and volcanic eruptions and cause your continents to split and sink in places and cause others to rise.

"We are VERY EXPERIENCED in the evacuation of populations of planets! This is nothing new for the galactic fleet! We expect to complete the evacuation on Earth of the souls of Light in fifteen minutes--even though they are of a tremendous number.

"We shall rescue the Souls of Light first. On our great galactic computers we have stored every thought, every act you have done in this and previous lifetimes. At the first indication of need to evacuate, our computers will lock onto the location of the Souls of Light where they are at that instant!

"After the Souls of Light have been evacuated, then the CHILDREN will be lifted off. The children are not old enough to be accountable, so they will be evacuated to special ships to be cared for until they can be reunited with their parents. There will be people specially trained to handle their trauma. Many may be put to sleep temporarily to help them overcome their fear and anxiety. Our computers are so sophisticated--far beyond anything on Earth in this age--and can locate mothers and fathers of children wherever they are and notify them of their safety. MAKE NO MISTAKE--YOUR CHILDREN SHALL BE LIFTED TO SAFETY DURING THE EVACUATION!

"After the evacuation of the children, the invitation will be extended to all remaining souls on the planet to join us. However, this will be for only a very short time--perhaps only fifteen minutes. There is no question of having enough space on board the ships for you, but because the atmosphere by this time will be full of fire, flying debris, poisonous smoke, and because the magnetic field of your planet will be disturbed, we will have to leave your atmosphere very quickly or we, also, with our spacecraft, would perish.

"Therefore, he who steps into our levitation beams first will be lifted first. Any hesitation on your part would mean the end of your third dimensional existence you call the physical body.

"Which brings us to the most serious and difficult part of the evacuation: As mentioned earlier, souls of Light have a higher vibration frequency than those who are more closely "tied" to the Earth and its ways.

"Since our levitation beams which will be lifting you off the surface of this planet are very close to the same thing as your electrical charges, those of low vibrational frequency may not be able to withstand the high frequency of the levitation beams without departing their third-dimensional bodies. If this happens, then your soul will be released to join our God, the Father. 'In His house are many mansions.'

"If you do not decide to step into the levitation beams to be lifted up, you might be one of the few who survive the 'cleansing' of the planet for the NEW GOLDEN AGE. However, during this period of cleansing, there will be great changes in climate, changes in land masses, as the poles of the planet may have a new orientation. This alone will create untold hardship for the survivors who may still not make it to the time of Radiance.

"The most important point for you to remember is this: Any show of fear lowers your frequency of vibration, thus making you less compatible with our levitation beams!!. Therefore: Above all else, REMAIN CALM. DO NOT PANIC. Know that you are in expert hands, hands which have extensive experience in evacuation of entire planets! WE CANNOT OVEREMPHASIZE THIS: REMAIN CALM! RELAX! DO NOT PANIC WHEN YOU STEP INTO OUR LEVITATION BEAMS. ABOVE ALL ELSE, MAINTAIN YOUR FAITH!

"What is to happen to you if you survive the lift off? First you will be taxied to our "mother ships" anchored high above the planet where you will be taken care of during your great trauma. Some of you may need medical attention. Our expert medical staff will be there to treat you with our highly advanced medical equipment. You will be fed and housed until such time as transfer elsewhere is advisable.

"Some of you will be taken to cities on other planets to be trained in our advanced technology before being returned to the planet Earth to start the time of Radiance.

"Your beautiful planet Earth is destined to be the most beautiful star in the universe. A planet of Light! Here, you will rejoin the remainder of the Universe in brotherly love and fellowship with God the Father.

"People of Earth: We love you!! Do not scoff at these words. As surely as the sun shines from the east to the west, so shall these things shortly come to pass!

"The cataclysms will begin WITHOUT WARNING! Everything will happen so fast, you will not have time to think! Think on these things NOW!

"Think; picture yourself standing with all the havoc around you, people screaming and running; others on their knees praying; automobiles crashing; glass breaking; buildings falling; ground shaking and gaping with huge cracks; debris falling all around you! THINK NOW!! WHAT SHALL I DO?? ANSWER: REMAIN CALM AND WITHOUT FEAR. MAINTAIN AN INNER PEACE OF MIND AND STEP INTO THE LEVITATION BEAMS WHICH FLOW FROM THE UNDERNEATH CENTER OF OUR SPACE CRAFT.

"As you are informed now as to what to do, spread the word to everyone you know. Be faithful to God! The time is very short! Perhaps we shall no longer be able to restrain the tilt of the Earth's axis, as we have been able to do with our energy beams and transmitters for the past several years.

"There is still a chance--a SLIGHT chance, that this great upheaval can be avoided. However, it will take extreme cooperation from you people of Earth--cooperation unlike you have ever exhibited before in this age.

"1. Avoid giving off negative energy through your distrust, greed, hatred and begin to help each other. By helping each other, you give off positive vibrations (energy). LOVE GOD! The positive energy in large mass will neutralize the weight of negative energy which has built up around the pole of your planet--this could keep it from tilting if enough positive energy is received in time. Your planet is a living organism. Send mental positive energy by thanking the Earth for all its bountifulness you have received.

"2. By whatever peaceful means at your disposal put sufficient pressure on your government(s) to permit us to land our spaceships on your planet and meet with your leaders and offer them our assistance and technology. WE WILL NOT DO THIS UNTIL WE ARE ASSURED WE WILL NOT BE TREATED WITH HOSTILITY OR BE INCARCERATED. With the cooperation of your world governments, we can greatly help you in more orderly evacuation of your planet, if indeed it still becomes necessary--which it may! If it does not then we can work together in the sharing of technology and live in brotherhood.

"WE HOPE YOU WILL TAKE THESE WORDS ON FAITH, BUT IF NOT, DO RESEARCH AND PROVE THEM TO BE TRUE FOR YOURSELVES. MEDITATE DAILY AND YOU WILL FIND AND KNOW THE TRUTH. PEACE BE WITH YOU."

At the conclusion of Yeorgos' program segment, Spotted Eagle again took center stage to make closing remarks and leave his special blessings with the group.

He told of the extreme importance of the upcoming Mighty Council Gathering and said elaborate plans had been made for its success. He told those gathered that under the facade of filming a motion picture, the meeting could take place uninterrupted by human interference. He said there would be many such activities taking place at various places on the planet in order to make the truth known. After the GATHERINGS there would no longer be doubts as to the existence of space brothers, and Earth man would know of the consequences he has brought upon himself. He said there would be other happenings which would also confirm the validness of these teachings.

He chanted his appreciation to the group and to the "GRANDFATHER" and the lights were extinguished. The canyon was once again silent.

PLATE VIII

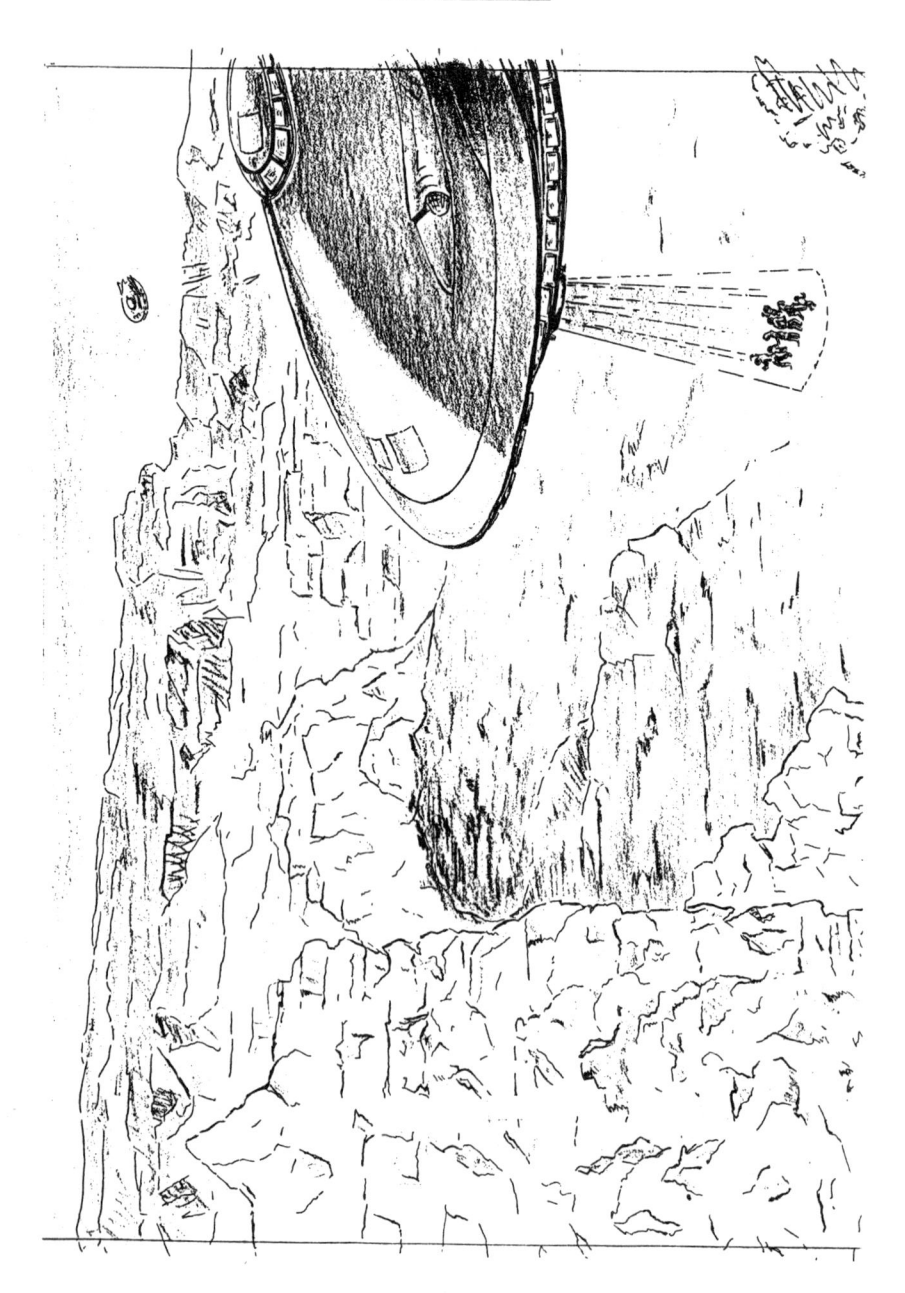

OPENING THE GATHERING

As the first gray fingers of light sifted silently across Bob's pallet he thanked GOD for the new day. He got up from his bed and dressed with eagerness. Today was the day of the Mighty Council Gathering and he felt as if he might explode from anticipation. He would dress as quickly as possible and walk over to the ship and have breakfast with his friends. Fawn had said she would be unable to see him before mid-morning and he was too restless to wait alone. He heard no sounds from outside and he wondered where everyone might be. The Indians did a sunrise ritual every morning, but no one was out this particular morning. Well, he assured himself, the Medicine Man would be doing his morning greeting to the day so he slipped on his shoes and hurried outside. The stillness lay heavy on the canyon; there was no Medicine Man and there were no Indians anywhere. Only the hawk was there dancing its own morning ritual. His heart clutched tightly as he thought of Fawn and wondered where she might be.

Bob was pondering the situation as he reached the space craft, changed his shoes and boarded. Things were "normal" as far as he could determine and he was somewhat relieved. Yeorgos was the first to greet him and smiled in response to his inquiries. He assured Bob that Fawn would be joining them for the journey to the GATHERING but the other tribal members had departed earlier. Others began to filter into the room and the subject was changed.

As promised, about mid-morning Fawn appeared. When Bob asked where she had been he received no answer and a wave of anxiety swept through him. He knew he was not ready to experience the sipapu, and sadness crossed him as he feared the time was very near for decisions to be made. He tried to put it from his mind and turned his thoughts to the GATHERING. The present group was unusually quiet and there was practically no conversation. Each was totally preoccupied with the anticipated Council meeting.

The silence continued during the swift journey to the meeting site. The craft sat down quietly behind a range of mountain foothills, shielded from Tehachapi. The travelers transferred into vans for the trip into town so as not to draw undue attention. They would simply appear to be more "participants" in the movie production.

There was a beehive of activity as they reached the filming location. Stands of bleachers had been erected to facilitate seating several hundred people and were almost filled. Camera crews were working diligently setting up backup lighting and generators to power the portable cameras. Stage crews were finishing the podium. About two to three hundred feet to the east of the stage area was a replica of a space ship identical to Yeorgos'. This was to be a major "prop" for the movie. The movie had been set up as a science fiction fantasy to avoid any questions or public attention. Plans had been carefully laid to the most minute details. Arrangements had even been made with the Air Force at Edwards Air Base to anticipate radar blips from "special effects". Bob smiled when he noticed several Air Force officers in the group of onlookers.

The town was full of visitors and town residents as it was in the middle of their annual Mountain Festival. It had been planned so that the local people could come to the meeting as "extras" and appear as audience members in the movie. There was great excitement in the town and it was as if everyone was on holiday. The stars in the movie were the most prominent in the industry and it was, in fact, a fantastic "happening" for the local residents. It had also pulled in many visitors which helped in the success of the Festival activities.

The invited participants had mostly come by car from Los Angeles, Lancaster, Mojave and Bakersfield, or had been brought in by private planes to the little airport. Tehachapi was too small to house very many overnight visitors.

As the group reached the bleacher area, Bob and the Hensleys were stunned. They had been told what was taking place and yet were totally unprepared for what they saw before them. The seats were filled with well known public figures from every walk of life. Faces which appeared at every peace gathering were present. Diana audibly gasped and Steve simply said "wow". Whoever set up this plan and script must surely have received the instructions from the Masters themselves, thought Bob. Fawn was totally serene and calm and Bob marveled as he watched her. She actually "glowed" and he wondered if anyone in the stands could see the aura surrounding her. He was hopelessly in love with her.

The sound from the bleachers was a vibrant buzzing as the people were deep into conversations. They were thrilled at the opportunity to be together and the consensus of feelings was that the movie would be a great positive boost to the various peace groups. Some who simply volunteered their time and paid their own transportation had to be refused participation due to the overwhelming turnout. Places were made for all in the observer area, however. There was plenty of room for any who wished to sit on the ground or stand around the periphery of the "scene" location, and all vacant spots were rapidly occupied. This was surely a day which would never be forgotten!!!

Steve noted that there was a heavy, dark cloud-bank rising above the hills to the northeast and moving directly toward the crowd. He said with great humor how wet it might become within a few hours and hoped the "show" might be finished before the downpour began.

The group found their appointed seats in the chairs which had been reserved near the stage in front of the bleachers. Yeorgos, Richard, Hypcos, John and Athenia had been seated to the right of and immediately adjacent to the stage. Several of the Indians from the canyon village were already gathered in seats close by Yeorgos' group. Bob wondered how they had traveled and supposed a second ship had brought them. His mind was boggled by his recent experiences and the things he had learned. It was as if it could hold no more and had begun to simply absorb instead of "react". Steve and Diana seemed to be accepting things far better than he, and Fawn was simply one with the energies that overwhelmed the setting. Bob looked to the northern sky and motioned Steve; the ominous cloud was becoming steadily more threatening.

Softly, through the buzzing of the crowd, came the strains of exquisite music. It seemed to have no place of origin, it simply wafted within the breeze. There was, however, an immediate reaction from the crowd. Not a human sound was audible; other than the music, silence was total. Then there was a gust of gentle wind through the set and the music became stilled; the crowd remained silent.

As if through some strange magic, figures began to move onto the stage as if from nowhere. They were obviously participants in the Council and were to be speakers, Bob presumed. As the speakers took their places and settled in their chairs, the vibration energy could be physically experienced as if it were electric currents. The set was intensely lighted but Steve pointed out that the auxiliary lamps were not functioning. The lighting crews were frantic in their efforts to get them turned on. The power had been interrupted and the electric lines were dead. The camera crews were making futile efforts to start the standby generators, but failed. The cameras, however, continued to function perfectly as if nothing were amiss. Some faces in the crowd began to show fear and Bob wondered if there might be panic starting. The entire setting was one which would make Spielberg grin with success; and that was obviously what was saving the situation from chaos--the crowd was still under the impression they were acting in a motion picture! There began a few murmurs from the crowd and, as if cued by the sound, John rose and strode to the podium; the light moved with him. The crowd was again hushed; the clouds moved ever closer.

John spoke softly, although his voice carried clearly to the most distant listeners. The electronic speaker system was dead but no-one noticed.

The cloud cover completely overlaid the area and continued its steady march to the south. It would soon blot out the sun; already there was an ominous darkness which caused a general feeling of strange tenseness.

Suddenly, as if someone had thrown a switch, John and the platform were bathed in a magnificent rainbow of colored lights. The lights, with their myriad of colors, flashed and danced a moment before settling into a thirty foot circle of intense spectrum of colors. One couldn't see beyond the brightness to find the source of the light; it simply came from somewhere in the sky overhead.

John radiated gentleness and love as he softly spoke. He said that this GATHERING was of such importance that all must listen carefully to the things which would be offered. He said the occurrences of this day would affect the universe. He said that apart from this GATHERING there would be happenings of such magnitude, within a period of these few days, that all Earth people would be forced to take note. He said that many things had been set in motion within the Earth itself, of which the consequences were irreversible. He emphasized that those gathered together at this place were not here by accident or coincidence; it was intended so that they would be safe in the physical body for further activities. He said that no one was to be afraid; all was as planned by the Higher Energies. At these words a calmness seemed to pass through the crowd. He continued by saying that most of those gathered here were part of the Ultimate Source's one hundred and forty-four thousand chosen teachers as spoken of through the mellenia of time past.

He said Earth had reached the final crisis and that the path taken from this point forward would decide the outcome of man's survival or self destruction. He said no one could act for another; all actions, changes, desires and choices must be made within the inner souls of each individual entity. He said these teachings had been handed down through the many ages of time and had recently been presented in modern language in the book *New Teachings*. In addition, the ancient teachings of ones in the oral tradition are to be presented for the first time in a new book called *The Sacred Hill Within*. Those would be available to all who would seek learning and knowledge.

He then stood silently for a moment, his face raised into the rainbow of brightness. When he returned his attention to the gathered audience, it was as if he held the colors within his physical hands--gently and with intense love.

He said each ray was precious just as each individual entity is precious to God, and that each is created from that single ultimate source of light--The God Light. Without that light, there would be no rainbow--there would be nothing. He described that Ultimate Light as being of such brilliance that no earthly entity could look into it. He said that from the Ultimate God Energy flowed two major Rays: one Ray being the Silver-White Ray of Creation and the other being the Golden-White Ray of the Christ purity. As these two magnificent Rays of Light merge and refract through the wondrous crystals of the universe, the light is splintered into the marvelous colored light energies of the rainbow.

But, he continued, no energy, no entity or even spirit source is to receive the Ultimate Reverence--that Ultimate Reverence is due only unto the Ultimate Light Source, GOD! That Light is the ALL and without that Light all else could not exist. He said all must cleanse their inner beings, love and care for each other, cleanse and heal our Mother Earth and give UNQUALIFIED love and reverence to that Ultimate GOD Light.

He said if man would not change and continued to turn from the Light toward darkness, the negative consequences would be absolute. Then, as if to make a point, he turned his face again into the light and raised his hands toward heaven. "No thing can survive without the Light," he repeated. As suddenly as the bolt of lightening which streaked instantly from the heavens, and with a horrendous burst of thunder, the world was plunged into darkness--total, absolute blackness.

It seemed an eternity locked in the void of nothingness, not even the tiniest spark of light shown from anywhere--the void was infinite. God had made his point for ever more. Bob could hear soft sobbing sounds around him but mostly there was only silence--the silence of death itself.

Then, John held forth one tiny match with its puny flame, the impact was total. And John spoke again and reminded each that we must take our own small flame, add it to our brother's and bring light and love again unto Earth or it would terminate in the darkness. The scene was once again slowly bathed in the rainbow colored light rays which then blended into two and then into the one brilliant Source of Pure White Light.

John then turned to Spotted Eagle and asked him to come forward. He introduced Spotted Eagle and said he was of the Ancient Ones. He said they were of the Beginning and their Truths had not changed throughout eternity. Some of the people had forgotten the Truths but they were there none-the-less; unchanged, and would now be remembered in order to lead us home.

MOTHER EARTH AND THE ANCIENTS

Spotted Eagle rose and greeted GOD after which he turned to the crowd and began to unfold his message:

"Standing atop Bear Butte my eyes gazed out over the lands far below my vantage point. The wind blew in from the North and all about me everything was in movement, along with my spirit. It was a very special time for me--for this was the time of my seventh vision quest. It had been a long and lonely journey this time for my spirit and me for the pathway lay hidden; covered over by the failings of all those who came this way in more recent times. But so few are aware of the proper reasons. The grandfathers sang on this night and the thunder of their drums rumbled across the darkened skies eventually fading away far off into the distant universe. Suddenly I was lifted------"

THE BEGINNING: "It sounds like the start of a wonderful story. A story about America's favorite pastime--American Indians. And in particular, it sets the scene for what so many feel to be the ultimate experience--a vision quest--which somehow will bring knowledge.

"A vision quest, a magnet for those digging into the Indian world. The unexplained need of these searchers to experience this mystic act or at best, know all that there is to know about this ancient ritual. As if knowing about this 'thing' will somehow change their lives and bring magical powers and much needed knowledge to their beings.

"But as you know, the vision quest is only one of the seven sacred rites of the Lakota People. There are other rites that go to make us a whole and complete People, but that is for another time. What we are to talk about now is what came in the vision quest for one human being, and how that vision can now be shared with all people.

"I am Little Crow, a Dakota/Lakota, born in the year 1933, making this birth the 198,000th incarnation of my spirit. Returning to this Earth plane only to share an infinite message with all life forms at the proper time. Permission to do so came during the early morning hours of January 5, 1987. To set the stage for this event were twenty-two strikes of lightening ending at exactly 2:22 a.m. In this life my spiritual number is a twenty-two (22). And away we go!"

THE SHARING: "I share with you now the following information as it has been given to me to 'only remember' over these many life times. I do not feel the need to support any of this information with any other written data or readings. For the source of this information is the same for everyone. This source as we shall refer to it has ALWAYS BEEN AND WILL ALWAYS BE. WITH NO BEGINNING AND NO END. IT EXTENDS OUT BEYOND ITSELF AND COMES BACK TO FORM THE SACRED CIRCLE. INFINITY--!"

THE MESSAGE: "We are travelers from unimagined regions of the universe with homelands in many places. This planet and the surrounding ones are the most recent stopping off places in this current vibrational form. Once more to act out the responsibilities of our selective realities, those being to accept who we are. No more ! No less!

"Our ability to travel is determined by our faith and nothing more. For all of the progress we've made on this place, we are still only able to move the physical properties of our being. It is sometimes hard to imagine our first journey to this place, this Mother Earth. I have come from the seven star system to this place, from Pleiades."

GOD: "To the many peoples of this planet there has been offered hundreds of explanations of the whose, what's, where's, and the why's of God. Different religions have fought countless battles over who's truths should be accepted. Millions of souls have been forced into unnecessary vibrational changes in the name of God and conversions. Countries and lands have been stolen and destroyed in the name of God.

"Leaders (as they call themselves) have ranted and raved throughout our brief history on this planet, forcing into our human mindset a system of fear and guilt. This guilt being so strong that humans had to devise various ways of escape, all self destructive and utterly confusing.

"Separation from the concept of God became the reality of the human being. Removal from center of the source of all things left mankind struggling and blinded by age old analogies concerning God. Many came among the people pulling them in separate groups, turning them one against the other, using the written word to convince them of their superiority of one over the other. Darkness reined and reins yet!

"There are examples upon examples and we could go on forever, seeing, on the passing screen, all that has occurred and the effect that these things have had upon the entire and related universe. The answer has always been simple and within our grasp, if only we were willing to take responsibilities of our creative spirits.

"You are of God and God is of you! The existence of God is only possible by our own existence. The maximum power of God at any one time is only in direct ratio to the numbers who have accepted their responsibilities of living within this concept. There was no beginning and there is no end, WE (GOD) have been and will be forever. We as human kind will exist in this vibrational form only as long as it takes for us to realize our responsibilities and our ultimate powers."

DIMENSIONS: "There are no dimensions where any one object, thing, act, person, religion, is better than any other. By this we mean that no one is more spiritual, more religious, more saved, less saved, more sinful, less sinful, than anyone else. No one thing is more or less inclined to receive any greater reward than any other thing.

"Dimensions have only been a creation of mankind, and a pretty screwed up one at that. What it has done is to serve as a fuel for the fires of ignorance, hatred, greed, destruction, and all of those wonderful things which we as human beings continued to hold up for our children to emulate. This has forced them to run faster and faster, all in pursuit of golden idols, running from God instead of towards God.

"We are all from the same source, we are that source; we are the God we seek. How can we not see the simplicity of this fact? We seek outside of ourselves what is within.

"No one is better or worse--we are the same, only in other forms. The time has now come to remove all of the stupid man made barriers to the pathways of acceptance and balance. There were no dimensions created by God--only those we have created against ourselves. WAKE UP, DUMMIES!"

RELATIONSHIPS: "We are related to each other and everything that ever has been or that will ever be. It is not only in the spiritual connection of which we speak, but it also refers to our physical connections as well.

"This is to say that each and every thing that we do effects and affects everything else within the universe to the same degree that things which occur in the universe effects or affects our current vibrational forms. This, in simplest terms, means that we are RESPONSIBLE to everything else for each and everything that we think or do. This is surely similar to the overall responsibility that we mistakenly attempt to put upon the shoulders of the mythical man-made God that we have necessity in creating.

"Everything is your relative and your responsibility. That is all and nothing more! (By the way, there are no greater rewards for anyone who comes to this conclusion, only discomfort and fitful nights of restless sleep.) So put aside all of the self indulging misconception that God created man to rule over anything or anyone. This has been one of the main stumbling blocks to our being able to remember just who and what we are. SO STOP PREACHING 'DIVISION' NONE SENSE and let's get on with the business at hand--our responsibilities as God--to the rest of our relatives."

RESPONSIBILITIES: "We have brought the world and its relative, the entire universe, to the point of destruction: self-destruction! When the big bang goes down it won't be because of the Russians, the Arabs, or anyone else. It will be because of our own selves. Nothing more and nothing less!!

"There are no outs no scape-goats! There are no fall guys and no more 'saviors' to die for us. (Boy, how long have we kicked that one around?) Now it is down to just us--you and me, folks. We did it and we have to clean it up, stop it, change it, or let it go as is. No one, and let me put this in Earth terms: 'no one but no one is going to come down from anywhere and save our assets.'

"Our brothers and sisters from the far reaches of the universe have been watching us for some time now, and they are attempting to assist us in reaching some kind of balanced position from whence we can, at last, launch into some constructive and realistic efforts at resolvement. That is, if we let them do so. By now, we are so afraid of anything on our sophisticated but childish radar screens, that we're ready to blow anything and everything out of the unfriendly skies. How dumb can we be? And, how long do we intend to stay that way?

"Their advancements have been totally a result of their acceptance of the God Self and its relationship to their own individual being. They are attempting to come among us and remind us of our responsibilities to the make-up of our total selves. We are the universe and we are about to self-destruct.

"They are not coming to preach to us in the manner or sense that we have been in the most recent past or present. This present dimension junk has done nothing but keep us blinded and confused as to our real purpose. It has served to turn us outward against all things that don't act, think, look, or worship like we do. We have wasted so much time buried in all this nonsense that we have totally lost sight of our spiritual reality. Is it any wonder that our prayers are not heard--we are too busy praying for ourselves to even be able to respond. We become selfish, rude and worst of all, doubtful of our very beings. Is it any wonder that we haven't been able to remember anything of importance?"

THE NOW: "It is time for all of us to come together in the reality of our beings and return the Earth to the condition in which we found it. I give no consideration as to just when you got here, it remains your responsibility just as much as it is mine.

"What were the plans we had for handling all of the toxics and other things that we have created in the name of progress? We are clogging the roads and skies so badly that we're bumping into each other. Soon there will be no more room to fit even one more car, and yet, we continue to turn them out. Please don't waste conversation on the economics of `everything' argument--it doesn't matter anymore. What does make a difference is our ability to get ourselves together and correct what we have done; we can if we want to! But, it will call for all of us to come together and work out this dilemma.

"All colors of beings must accomplish this--it is the responsibility of all colors of beings. All mindsets of beings must come together and work together and all of us must come together NOW!"

THE FUTURE: "It will be just what we make it, not what we allow someone else to make it for us. No one can do it for you or for me. We are the ones that have to make the future a reality--not just an empty statement."

THE CONCLUSION: "There are no separations of beings, no one is going anywhere without the other. There are no better or worse beings, one to be shipped here and the other to go there; get it out of your head and get down to the task at hand.

"We come from the same place and to that place we shall, in time, return, but only after we have met our commitments and responsibilities--and not before; certainly not before anyone else because we've been a better Jew, Catholic, Christian, Pagan or anything else that we care to utilize in an attempt to try and slide by.

"For the total time of our creation, we have always looked for the easy out--for someone to come and do it for us. This time it won't work. It's up to us--it is our problem and we have to resolve it. It doesn't have a thing to do with how good you've been or how bad, but rather if you are capable of seeing the reality of God.

"We started together and together we will end--no one will finish before the other--so let's get to work and re-educate ourselves and our relatives.

"As the vision said, God will only exist when mankind accepts the fact that the spark within them is indeed the God-Self! I wish you well; maybe this time we can get it done. FOR ALL MY RELATIONS!"

THE MASTERS SPEAK

When Spotted Eagle had finished speaking, he was replaced by the other energies on the platform, one after another. There was hardly any motion in the crowd as each sat in rapt attention.

The next speaker introduced himself as Michael and began to speak.

"Now be at peace and be filled with joy. I enter into your midst to bring you tidings of what shall be. You are to be glad at that which you are receiving. The hour has come in which you will see that which has been prophesied. You may rejoice in this moment, you of planet Earth.

"You are to be the teachers and set down the things which shall be given to you. You will be the ones to make record of my words so that it might go out unto all the lands that all who hunger and thirst for the word shall have access unto it. So be it as it is given.

"Praise you your Lord, your God, your Creator for your Creator has given to you of the golden potion that you might be as one to drink thereof, and awaken with that which is seeing. You shall be as ones to come unto the table and truly, your eyes shall behold that which is placed before you. You have been as a fool for you have been invited, yet you have not tasted for you have not been as one to come. You did not come because you have not heard the call. You have not heard. NOW HEAR ME! LISTEN TO MY WORDS! My word is that which is given unto you by the Divine Principle, The Father GOD. Look not to one or another but look into that which is within your own breast, that you might manifest of your creation. Be you as one to hold your own destiny in your own hand, and know it is your own choice. So be it as it is given to you. Listen well to that which is spoken to you. Even in the quietness of your slumber is the Word sent to you.

"Hear with your ear the Word. Cleanse yourselves. Rid yourself of the iniquities of your flesh. Bless your place of dwelling and also those that dwell with you. Let your true inner self come forth. So be it. It will be for you to carry the Word. Blessings to all. Amen."

Gabriel next rose to speak:

"REJOICE! REJOICE! Lift your voices in thanksgiving. Your hour has come. Your deliverance is with you. You have been looking into the sky to see the Son's return. He is not there. He is about the Earth; he is with the Earth. He is with you; He has never gone from you; He is you! He walks with you and beside you; He is your brother; He is of Himself; He is you.

"I say to you, He is you for that which is your Divine Seed is as His Seed. He is come. The time of the fall has left you. You will be as ones to build the Golden City. You are the Ones. REJOICE! REJOICE! I say these things to you; I am Gabriel."

As Gabriel returned to his chair an audible sigh passed through the audience and Bob felt a shiver skip the length of his spine. Fawn slipped her hand into his and then sat motionless.

The next speaker took his place.

"I am known on Earth as the one who rides of the wind. I am Jophiel. You are the manifestation of the Breath of the Divine Principle. I will bend my knee and draw close to your ear that I may whisper the truth unto your ear. Look at what is about you. See and recognize that which is carried by the wind and which is within the air. See that which is happening for it shall be of the air, the waters, and the land. Look carefully at that which is occurring as your time of three is about you.

"As this is done about the land so shall you also be as the land, for you are like creation. Each of you is as the Child of Perfection. Recognize that which is given you as your mother Earth is about her birthing, so, too, are you. Give up that which is as the chain that ties you down. Vomit up that which is unclean from your lower portion. Give up that which is the lead in your bellies. Be released.

"Feel the new air. Drink the fresh water. Kiss the clean Earth that nourishes you. Offer up your thanksgiving and go forth to claim your reward. You will be ready to claim your reward for you shall be as one that has passed your testing. You shall be graduated. Your reward shall be tenfold that which you would think. And your reward will be TRUTH. And your reward will be ENLIGHTENMENT. You shall be as one to walk in Light, and you shall be as one to know of that which comes from your lips. You shall be ones who shall build of the Golden City. You will be the ones that bring forth the bricks and mortar. You will be the ones to plant the seeds and reap the harvest. You will be the music and your orchestra will be as the wind. The birds will add their voices to the chorus. You will create the perfect symphony, for you will have come from the brink of the pit, and will have been lifted up from your state of degradation. You shall be as the song of the Lords as you command of the wind. So be it as it is given and written. So be it evermore. Amen."

Silence.

"I am Raphael. I do hold unto the four corners of Earth's feeble plane. Your hour has come. You are of the birthing. You are of the pain of the birthing. Feel and know this is your time. Feel as the one that has nurtured you as she does writhe in her labour. Know you have come to give her that which is her measure of comfort in the hour of her anguish. Rejoice at your role. Rejoice that you have come for you have come of a great and precious service. The birthing is at hand. You are Light that shall cast away the darkness that all shall be Light for this Jewel of the Creation.

"You are the ones that shall cleanse the wounds. You must bind up the tears. You are the ones who shall gather the linen to wrap the new infant as it comes from the womb. You shall be the ones to proclaim that which is come. You shall be the ones to hold forth the new baby as the proud family that all might see who has come. You shall proclaim of this one so that all shall recognize who has come of the birthing. I am Raphael that speaks from the four corners of that which is Earth, for I carry of this one in the linen cradle that she might not be shifted in her hour. I do succor this one that she might be nourished as she is of her time of delivery. Do not look outside yourselves for a "SAVIOR"--none is there! Look within where the Truth of God resides and open your hearts, eyes and minds."

Next:

"All Hail! I am Chamuel who comes forth to give you a portion. It is that I do put forth the call that shall, from the north to the south, and from the east to the west that all might have the opportunity to know of the reckoning.

"Small ones of the Jewel, the emerald, wake up to your hour. Do not sleep on; it is your hour. Be one to cast your eye to the left and see of those that do choose not to hear the trumpet and arise. Be one who cast your eye to the right that you might see the works of your Creator. See you now as the lands rumble and boil. Watch as that which was sure is shaken beneath your boots. Now cast your eyes unto the front and see the skies as they quake and pour forth great cleansing. Look behind you, and see that which has been swept from you.

"Behold, I say to you to cast your eyes unto the skies above you and SEE! So be it."

Diana was visibly upset and Steve held her close. Slowly, reality begin to sift through the onlookers.

The next speaker began: "You weep and you moan at that which is your lot. I say it is of your own choosing to the last detail. I am Zadkiel and I say that you would rise up and say that this is the work of the Hand of the Creator. I say to you that it is not so; you have done it yourselves. You slumbered and have forgotten. Those who continue in their slumber will not see that which is their purpose. The Creative Principle shall not take up the burden which you gave fashioned for yourselves. You are the Creative Principle and you must carry the responsibility; you can not cast it upon another. You shall be given an awareness that you might see this Truth. You shall also be given a mind that will know of this.

"It is at this hour that you will see and feel. You will experience the power of that which has been given unto you. You will be as ones to see the purging and the bringing forth. You shall be the ones to see and proclaim that it is the works of the Divine Hand. You shall witness the boils as they spew forth their uncleanliness and impurities that have been gathered within the bowels of Earth. You shall see the waters as they rise up from their sleeping. You will see the waters come forth in swiftness to wash away that which has been placed upon the fallen alter. This shall be so. It is by my hand that it is wrought forth. The true shall see of the cleansing and you shall be as ones to lift up your voices in praise and thanksgiving. You shall witness the washings and the cleansings, and shall know that the hour of change has arrived. So be it evermore!"

As Zadkiel finished his portion he explained that he, as well as the others, had been called by many other "names" during the existence of time, and that names had no significance in the higher dimensions. He then turned to another speaker behind him and motioned him forward.

There was a bit of a pause and a few words were exchanged among the speakers. Bob and Steve took the opportunity to give attention to the sky overhead. It was darkened as if a solar eclipse were taking place. In addition, the Earth set up an almost constant pulsating trembling. Evidently an earthquake had taken place and was being followed by one upon another after shocks. The crowd began to chatter and, if they were not under the impression they were experiencing movie special effects, Bob and Steve were convinced there would be total panic and chaos. The first shock had been severe. Paul estimated it had to have been of a magnitude of at least four points. They knew it was not a pretend performance and they wondered what must be happening to the Pacific coastal areas. They had been warned that things would be frightening, but the warning did not prepare them for the feeling of total devastation that engulfed them. Diana was trembling but Fawn appeared totally serene.

Bob was relieved when the next speaker walked to the podium; it would distract the crowd before they realized that the "special effects" were real.

"I greet you, I am Uriel and I bless you with peace and beg of you not to be afraid. I come at this hour to offer you the Golden White Light which is your own Sacred Light. I say unto you that within the breast of each of you is the flame that waits to be ignited. Feel and experience the beloved joy of the touch of the angel's wing as the spark is given to you. Feel as you are released from your bondage to come forth in the Light and join into the Infinite Circle with your brothers. Be that which is your birthright. Manifest that which is your responsibility. Answer to none but your inner Divine Self. Do not bow your knee to a false image. Recognize that within you is your own link to the Perfect. Manifest that which you have come to be. Manifest that which you have as your own right, as your own portion.

"Some have not felt my nearness, of the spark that would give you knowledge. I would give that which would cause you to see what you are, who you are, and that you would be that which were created to be. The Lords of the Heavens come of this hour to give to you small ones assistance and allow you to open your inner selves and reach knowledge of yourselves. Do not fear us who come before you--we are only a reflection of yourselves. So be it evermore."

As Uriel spoke the Earth had given two terrible heaves of activity and the crowd was nervous. Michael hurriedly regained the podium.

"I was the first that did give to you instructions on this day, so shall it be that I shall be the last to say unto you that which will be given. About your heads you will feel of the Blue Light." And, as he spoke the words, a calmness swept over the audience and soft blue light seemed to settle about the area. "You shall feel of the strength that I give unto you. You shall be as ones to see your strengths, and you shall also be given to see the strength of others. You shall know each other and recognize your brotherhood. All must become as brothers if you are to survive. You must work to restore balance and harmony upon your nurturing sphere. Look beyond and see the works and find that which is buried. Yes, there will also be beauty and joy as you experience the growth and changing of this time.

"You shall be given of that which is yours of long past, if that is your choice. You shall be as ones to straighten your backs and walk with head erect for you shall be as ones of TRUTH.

"The road shall be made with a portion of smoothness for you have need to rest along the journey. But I say unto you, and I give to you that you shall not be ones to continue of the smooth road, for your journey requires much from you. You shall be as ones given of the TRUTH, yet you shall be as ones that must earn of the right that you would see of it. So be it. It is done.

"I, Michael, do place my seal upon this work. Truth Seeker, find you the WORD that is buried.

"This is finis and has gone unto the Cosmos that all might receive. Do not lay down your pen for the rest is yet to be written. I have now given this message and upon this word is placed my seal. Amen."

THE SPACE BROTHERS SPEAK

As Michael stepped back to his chair, John moved rapidly to the podium and began to speak. He explained that what would happen next, was in no way to be considered magic nor spiritual, as that word is defined in Earth terms. He said the next group of participants were not to be considered Gods, and more, that each present is to recognize the God Source within himself.

The demonstration would be to represent to Earth people that they are not alone; there are wiser and more advanced brothers in the outer realms which we call "space". He said they come in willingness to render assistance during Earth's time of crisis, cleansing and rebirthing. He said they would also explain that they come to evacuate Earth if that should eventually become a necessity. He said many of the Galactic Fleet commanders would present themselves; the first speaker would be the Supreme Commander of the Fleet, Ashtar.

All eyes were immediately riveted to the sky above; it seemed as if everyone present momentarily forgot the heaving Earth under their feet. The bleachers continued to tremble and vibrate.

Within seconds the boiling clouds began to vaporize and high, high above the Gathering was what appeared to be the under side of some monstrous craft. The periphery of the object was visible. It seemed to blanket the world. It appeared to be very distant above the Earth, which made its tremendous size more ominous.

From underneath the "object" suddenly appeared several smaller craft which were disc shaped and typical of descriptions of space ships. These ships gathered closely together and simultaneously brilliant beams of light appeared from the center of each craft. The audience gasped in shock as beings began to float downward through the beams. One by one they joined the speakers on the stage. Fleet Commander Ashtar immediately took the podium. The Earth continued its convulsions.

"I direct my thoughts to you of planet Earth that are the volunteers from throughout the Cosmos, from the angelic realms, and the representative of the Hierarchy. Each of you has passed through a period of great turbulence. You have felt the impact and the initial injury as lower energies have been unleashed to be removed from those that are about you. As you have grown in your own awareness and enlightenment, your vibrational pattern has altered, and you are, indeed, much more fragile than those ones that would choose to walk the path of oblivion. Constantly you are on our monitors, that we might send forth healing, in balancing, and allowing you to ride through this period of turbulence. This is brought to you for your time is not yet over. Earth, and those that are with her in these hours, are experiencing the throes, the anguish of the birthing process, so shall you feel of this within your being. As you take the opportunity to retreat into silence, into places of quietness, of solitude, so do you receive of that which will assist you in your healing and your balancing. We recognize the role you have selected is indeed one that is the front line of the great forces. We salute you in that which you have come to do, and we are humbled to serve with you at this time of Earth's crisis.

"As Earth makes preparation for moving into the next dimension, and you prepare in your assistance, you shall each, in your own way, receive increased enlightenment and awareness. Your whole vibrational pattern is being quickened. The hour of seeing, of knowing, of believing is upon you, that you might start as one small voice, and as you come together the voice shall grow, and you shall be heard throughout the planet.

"Our legion of volunteers, I put forth the call that the hour is nigh of awakening. We of the fleet salute you. We stand ever ready to offer assistance to you. You are the vital key for all ones of planet Earth. May I offer my most sincere appreciation to each of you for selecting the role that you have chosen. Know that we stand ever ready to assist you. PEACE."

Ashtar introduced the next speaker as Andromeda Rex.

"I am here to speak to you who are newly awakened. Many of you are experiencing great confusion at this hour. Many of you are feeling great loss, a great void. This is because of the new communication and the removal of lower energies. Some of you are frightened at the thought that a voice or a thought is entering into your field over which you have no specific control. It is a process of change and we will help you through your progression.

"Many of you will experience communication from other dimensions. This is not the role of ALL on planet Earth. Indeed, if all were to grow the seed then who would weave to make the garments? Or, if all of you were to grow the seed, then who would build the dwellings? Each will have your own unique role.

"As you become aware of your involvement with us, of your role, of your purpose, our communication with you will be more easily established. In order to facilitate this, I suggest that each of you designate the same period each day, that you would sit in quiet, in solitude, that your being, that which you call your body, might attune to this time frame, that you might learn to settle yourself, to clear your mind of its clutter, and to be ready to receive. We of the higher dimensions will continue to work closely with you."

Soltec took the podium.

"Greetings Earth friends, I am Soltec. I will speak of the geophysical manifestations that shall be appearing on Earth. Upheavals and eruptions will be seen about the planet. This condition shall be accelerated in the upcoming days, and indeed, as seasons change upon the Earth, the change shall bring forth great unbalance in the weather patterns, as well as the geophysical reactions to the change.

"Parts of the planet will experience flooding, tidal waves, excessive rain, mud slides, periods of great turbulence in weather patterns. As you of Earth consult your media, you will be unable to turn on your televisions or read your papers without some mention of a so-called disaster on Earth. This is an attempt to rid Earth of the negativity that she so long has held. This unbalanced energy is coming to the surface to be released, to be expelled from the heart of Mother Earth.

"This shall be a time, as seasons change, that these shall be altered. The season that you call spring shall be minimal, just as that season which you call fall. There shall be a 'sliding' from the extreme of summer to the extreme of winter, and from the extreme of that which you call winter into that which is called summer. The balmy times upon your planet shall begin to minimize as the weather patterns react to that which is being released from Mother Earth and those of you that are with her.

"We have placed a belt of ships around the center of Mother Earth to assist in her stabilization. Also, we have stationed at each of the polar areas large magnetically-controlling ships to assist in the stabilization from that view. We will continue these efforts to, hopefully, prevent further wobbling or unbalance of Earth on her axis as these changes progress. We do not know, at this point, how long a period of time we can maintain the present balance.

"As the severities increase there will be a shortage of food supplies as you recognize them. Plants will be introduced in various locations on your planet which shall be discovered and use shall begin. I offer encouragement and I share freely of that which I have available."

The Earth movements had lessened in frequency as the next speaker took the floor.

"Keil-Ta is my name and I will discuss our ships. Our particular portion of the command has been assigned in the area of evacuation and lift off. This is why we now make our presence known. Our ships are not of the shape with which most Eartheans are familiar, ours is an oblique disc. And those of you that might have seen it as it has traveled through the atmosphere might have mistaken our light pattern for one of a shooting star, or a falling star as you would say. Our ships do not have to conform to a specific pattern for navigation because the ethers of our galaxy are of such an attunement that they present no resistance as we go forth.

"During this period our smaller scout ships shall be very close to Earth and we will be easily visible. Our purpose will be to become even more familiar to you of Earth to ease your fears should evacuation become necessary."

Keil-Ta was replaced by one he introduced as Beatrix.

"Greetings. I am here to speak to you who are architects, physicists and biochemists. You must now find new answers that do not take away from, but rather contribute to. Man of Earth has felt he has accomplished a great deal as he split the atom. Indeed, he has accomplished far more than he realizes. For, by splitting the atom of the living elements, he has indeed speeded up the hands of the clock. As one atom of one living element feels of its unbalance, so do all living atoms throughout the Cosmos feel of this unbalance, also. You noted ones of science have overlooked the magnetic pull of the Earth, of the ley lines that are about Earth. You have overlooked the use of the crystal. You have overlooked the use of various gem stones that are found about your planet. These long forgotten knowings shall come to the surface for ones of this day. And ones in places of your university settings, and those areas of your businesses and your companies that employ others for their ability to think and reason, shall come together in a mutual sharing toward enlightenment. Man's first realization will be that of the undoing he has created by splitting the atom. You must rethink your way of living.

"Scientists of your great nations must come together to share knowledge and expertise. You must learn to share without external influences of your political governments. You must speak as brothers. You must build a peaceful environment or you cannot survive."

The feeling of restlessness seemed to begin to unnerve the audience as the realization of the reality of the moment began to take hold. One known as Algaron quickly rose to speak.

"We must turn our attention to the severe problems you face with health and nutrition on Earth. There will be great cleansing of Earth and souls are going to rapidly be removed from your planet. You will find illness widespread. There will be no earthly cure for these illnesses. This has already begun with the introduction of that which is known to you of Earth as AIDS. You will continue to also experience that which is known to you as cancer. There will be a widespread increase in those diseases caused by the lower energy forms; those such as AIDS and other forms of venereal diseases.

"Do not despair as the general health for light workers shall actually be increased. Many alternate sources of foods rather than the animal proteins will become most familiar. Many ones will try the new plants and find ways to prepare these that shall be most palatable to all of you. This will be a great time of regaining balance and attunement for those of you known as light workers. We will be constantly with you to assist you in any way possible."

One known as Monka replaced Algaron.

"I will be brief as I see you are restless and frightened. You must realize that the strength and harmony which you seek is within your own beings. There shall continue to be unbalance. There shall continue to be countries and leaders that will test the patience of all the world. The acts of terrorism will be a manifestation of this. It will sometimes appear that you are on an unavoidable path to a great and mighty war. But we shall not allow this war to be.

"Yes, the hold will be most tenuous, but war shall not pervade on planet Earth. The councils, the tribunals have come together in one great and mighty auspicious gathering. And the Decree has gone forth, planet Earth shall not be destroyed. And those that are of the Light shall not be denied their birthright. Thank you and I salute the volunteers on Planet Earth."

Hatonn speaks:

"The Light Forces of all Creation are coming together in assistance of this jewel within the Cosmos. Be strong in these upheavals of Earth. Recognize that there are those who cannot see beyond this moment and shall cry of catastrophe and calamity. They shall cry of great terribleness of all the acts that are coming about. Know as this is done that these see with a very myopic eye. Always look beyond the moment. Look to the Divine Purpose. We work toward the Universality of all man-kind. We are your brothers. Salu Salu Salu."

THE SACRED CIRCLE--THE CHRIST

A gasp swept through the viewers as the next entity seemed to float to the front of the platform--it appeared to be only an energy essence.

"I Am that which does awaken within the heart cell of mankind. I AM THE CHRIST ENERGY. I Am the totality of the at-one-ment with the Perfect Principle, the Divine Principle. I Am the sum of each of the parts that is the totality, that is the sum. I Am the voice that is within the heart of each, and yet I Am the voice that is the totality.

"As I receive, as I am quickened, I come forth within the mighty temple as a great and a mighty flame, that is a consuming flame within each one. I speak not as a hallowed station that is beyond the reach, that lies just beyond their fingertips. Nay, I am not there. I Am within thy heart, and I ask to be heard. I Am thy Divinity. I Am thy Christhood.

"You have traveled the path that has been one of darkness. You have traveled as ones alone. And as the call goes forth no longer shall you be as ones lone, for you shall see of Me in the eye of another. And that which is the Christ within you shall mingle with the Christ that is of your brother, that the greater portion might come forth. The hour of recognition has been called. It is now that each has been touched within their heart cell to allow Me to come forth, to consume the vessel, to lead of the portions, to mold yet a new form.

"I Am the Christ. I Am that which is known as the Son, and I dwell within each, and I Am of All. Do not mistakenly think that you can place any name upon my being so that I might bear a label of your making. I have been as the sleeping giant that has waited most patiently to awaken. And it is now that I have been touched, and I stir within your breast as I awaken from my slumber, as I rise up from my cot to lead you in the New Day. I Am within your breast, and I am within the breast of all mankind. You have but to recognize of Me and that which I do in the Name of Yahweh. Within your breast shall I manifest the glories which you are, which I AM. Within me do I come forth to give unto you that which is your right and inheritance. Within you I do stir to awaken you to your portion, I do awaken you to come forth to be as you were created.

"I sleep no longer, for I have been touched and I stir in my awakening, and I yearn that I might come forth to consume you in your totality, in your realization of who you are. I Am of the Creative Principle. I Am the seed cell that is your beginning. I Am totality. I give to you the Breath of Life. I awaken that you might manifest that which you came to be. I Am the Christ. I AM!"

CLOSING THE GATHERING

As the energy of The Christ seemed to simply cease to exist, John moved forward to make closing remarks. Bob noted that the other "spiritual" speakers were no longer on the platform. He has not seen them leave, but even Spotted Eagle was gone. Only the "space brothers" remained.

As he was pondering this a commotion in the sky caught his attention. Several beams shot down into the audience and some elderly appearing persons ascended up the light beams. John continued speaking as if there was nothing unusual about people traveling through a beam of light.

He thanked the group for attending the meeting. He again urged the group to have no fear of the changes which were occurring. He said the GATHERING has been set up in this manner to insure safety for all the brothers from outer dimensions. He said it had been extremely important that there be no misrepresentation of what had been presented. He continued by encouraging that no one despair at what would be made known to them shortly, that it was part of the cleansing process and that the ones attending had been brought here for their safety. They were to go now and aid their fellow humans who would be in great trouble at that very moment, from the changes which had taken place during the duration of the meeting. He reassured everyone that there would be continual help available from the other dimensions.

Just as he was calling God's blessings upon the GATHERING, there came an abrupt rumble and jolt to the area. Many in the crowd had gotten to their feet immediately following the quake and confusion began to move through the people. A woman a few seats in front of Bob lost her balance and he rushed to assist her. The world had suddenly turned upside down. He turned back to Steve and Diana but they were not there. A feeling of desolation passed through him as he realized that Fawn, too, was gone.

MIRACULOUS RESCUE

The scene was one of frantic activity as travelers came upon the accident and stopped to render aid. The first to stop were two men and a woman. They were traveling in a four-wheel driven vehicle with a winch attached to the front. One man and the woman rushed down the embankment toward the river. The man immediately scrambled into the water and began to work at freeing Diana. The woman stood by to render first aid. The second man seemed to analyze the situation and, as he started for the river, released the winch mechanism and dragged the tow cable along with him. Within moments, Diana was pulled to the shore and the woman began working over her. The first man was trying to release Steve from the driver's seat, but was unable to unfasten the seat belt. The second man hurriedly attached the cable to the rear of the convertible.

A second vehicle had stopped on the road above. A lone man started down the incline. The second man called to him with some instructions pursuant to running the winch. He got into the truck, started the winch and began lifting the convertible from the water. As soon as Steve's head was above the water the first and second men worked him free of the belts. The lone driver then rushed down the hillside to do whatever he might to help. The second man was working with Steve. At this time, Diana had begun to show weak signs of life but was completely disoriented and could not maintain consciousness. Steve did not respond to the CPR being rendered by the three men present.

Two more vehicles had stopped above on the highway. One shouted down that he had a two-way and had called for assistance. He would stay by the radio for communication. In the second vehicle was an Indian family. All slid down the embankment to join those working with Steve and Diana.

Unnoticed by the crowd which had gathered, the Indian man quietly slipped away from the group and walked a few feet up the river, stopped, and looked about him. He saw nothing other than a hawk making its incessant circles in the air. He meditated for a while then turned back to the crowd. It seemed an interminable period of time before ambulances arrived but in the interim Steve had begun to show some evidence of life. The three men continued to work feverishly. By the time the ambulances and paramedics arrived both victims were coming around although Steve showed no signs of regaining consciousness.

More than an hour passed before the scene cleared and returned to normal. Those who had stopped to assist stood around and conversed for a while then went their separate ways. They left the hawk to his lonely vigil.

In the late afternoon a car stopped and the Indian made his way back down to the river. It was as if some unknown messenger had summoned his return.

The Indian sat silently for several minutes lost in his mind. Suddenly there came the screech of the hawk as it swept low over the Indian's head and glided into the side canyon. The Indian appeared to almost become one with the bird. He rose to his feet and made his way directly to a shallow crossing in the river. He turned and signaled to someone waiting in the car, to summon help. He then jumped from rock to rock until he reached the far side of the water. Then, without pausing, he headed directly to the place where the hawk had vanished. The car drove away to seek help and left the Indian alone with the canyon.

The hawk had come to rest on the rock outcropping up the small canyon, waiting. It had perched above the drawing of a beautiful Indian maiden with birds circling her head and shoulders. The Indian smiled a knowing smile. He walked faster as if drawn by some unseen magnet to the base of the painting. There at the base of the painting, in a deeply washed out hole, lay the crumpled unconscious body of Bob.

When the helicopter arrived there was only the broken body of Bob and a lone Indian man. There was no wall painting, neither was there a hawk. When the men and machinery departed there was only silence once again in the canyon.

IT WOULD BE A LONG WHILE BEFORE BOB, DIANA OR STEVE WOULD REALIZE THEY KNEW ALL THOSE WHO HAD STOPPED TO HELP.

PLATE IX

FROM HERE?

When Bob finally opened his eyes he had no idea where he might be. He could see that he was in a hospital room but couldn't remember why he would be there. He searched his memory and slowly, bits and pieces of the accident came forth. He could remember the accident and he could remember being in terrible pain. It was confusing, however, as he recalled the severe pain coming from his left arm--it had been unbearable. In his mind he could recall a lot of blood and broken bones--and always the terrible pain.

He was alone in the room and he carefully checked himself as thoroughly as possible. His left arm was tender to the touch but was certainly not broken. There was evidence of a freshly healed wound of some sort; he could not remember any incident which would have produced the scar. He wondered how long he had been unconscious. It seemed many things were missing from his memory but the recent happenings were vivid. In his mind he could see Diana and Steve in the river and painful sadness swept over him. He rang the bell for the nurse.

A team of nurses and a doctor rushed into the room and began working over him. They were full of smiles and assured him that he was doing very well; they had been concerned for a few hours though, the doctor said. They assured him further that the accident had happened only two days before. But what about the arm? The doctor said they had assumed he had been in a separate, recent accident because several recent injuries were noted in many places on his body. Bob felt completely confused. The doctor also said that his friends would be ecstatic to hear of his regaining consciousness. "But--they are dead," he murmured. "No," was the response, "they were pulled from the river and are doing very well!" In fact Diana had been released after overnight observation and Steve would probably be discharged within a day or so. Bob wondered what was happening to his mind.

It was a joyous reunion later that day when Bob was wheeled into Steve's room. They were to share the room until discharge.

Diana was full of giggles and chatter. It was good to simply be alive. Bob was in a bed nearest the window and had a view of the parking lot. There, perched on a light pole, was his beloved hawk.

It was late afternoon when two men and a woman were ushered into the room. They were very friendly and greeted the three "patients" warmly. They explained that they had been among the ones who had pulled Steve and Diana from the river, and apologized to Bob for having overlooked his presence. They said they were simply checking on their health and were on their way out of town. Addresses and phone numbers were exchanged, and promises were made to stay in touch. Steve, Bob and Diana did not recognize Yeorgos, Hypcos and Athenia.

As Bob watched his hawk preen atop the light pole, he also absentmindedly watched an Indian and two other men conversing with a beautiful nurse. Then she accepted a bouquet of flowers and a parcel, waved good-by and all dispersed. It was Fawn, Spotted Eagle, John and Richard, but Bob didn't know.

A half hour or so later the nurse pushed through the door and came into the room. She said the flowers and box had been left for all three. She said the people had helped in the rescue and sent the things with best wishes. She placed the flowers between the beds and handed the box to Diana. The card was inscribed "Best wishes for a speedy recovery and hope to see you again. Your River Friends". Bob could hardly pay attention to Diana; he could not take his eyes from the nurse--then he realized he could not recognize her.

The three were completely confused by what was in the parcel. There were books, one entitled *New Teachings* and the other *The Sacred Hill Within*. Then there were engineering papers with drawings. One was of a small vibration box attached to the bottom of a wind turbine. the turbine was identical to the ones being installed by the three in Tehachapi. The other drawing was of a device with crystals and gold wires. It appeared to be drawings of an invention of Nikola Tesla which the three had been researching. There seemed to be at least one important element missing from the drawings, however. Then there was the pocket change from Bob's pocket along with his pocket knife; there was also a beautiful arrowhead with the point missing. The remainder of the contents of the box were equally confusing. Among them were three packets of seeds; sprout seeds, soy beans and lentils. The fourth packet contained a green powdery substance and was labeled "algae". There were instructions for cultivation included.

As the three puzzled over the contents of the package and speculated about what might be the meaning, the nurse set about taking Bob's temperature and vital signs in a routine way. Bob still could not take his eyes from her face. Then, as she bent over him to apply the blood pressure cuff, a pendant around her neck swung free--the point from a beautiful arrowhead was mounted in a setting of gold.

The hawk screeched his cry and lifted into the sky.

BOOK LIST

THESE WORKS ARE A SERIES CALLED THE **PHOENIX JOURNALS**. THEY HAVE BEEN WRITTEN TO ASSIST MAN TO BECOME AWARE OF LONGSTANDING DECEPTIONS AND OTHER MATTERS CRITICAL TO HIS SURVIVAL AS A SPECIES. JOURNALS ARE $6.00 EACH PLUS SHIPPING & HANDLING [See order form for charges].

1. SIPAPU ODYSSEY ISBN 1-56935-045-0
2. AND THEY CALLED HIS NAME IMMANUEL, I AM SANANDA ISBN 1-56935-014-0
3. SPACE-GATE, THE VEIL REMOVED ISBN 1-56935-015-9
4. SPIRAL TO ECONOMIC DISASTER ISBN 0-922356-07-6
5. FROM HERE TO ARMAGEDDON 1-56935-043-4
6. SURVIVAL IS ONLY TEN FEET FROM HELL ISBN 0-922356-11-4
7. THE RAINBOW MASTERS ISBN 1-56935-017-5
9. SATAN'S DRUMMERS ISBN 1-56935-054-X
10. PRIVACY IN A FISHBOWL ISBN 1-56935-042-6
11. CRY OF THE PHOENIX ISBN 1-56935-036-1
12. CRUCIFIXION OF THE PHOENIX ISBN 0-922356-41-9
13. SKELETONS IN THE CLOSET ISBN 0-922356-15-7
14. RRPP* *RAPE, RAVAGE, PLUNDER AND PILLAGE OF THE PHOENIX ISBN 0-922356-16-5
15. RAPE OF THE CONSTITUTION ISBN 0-922356-17-3
16. YOU CAN SLAY THE DRAGON ISBN 0-922356-21-1
17. THE NAKED PHOENIX ISBN 0-922356-22-X
18. BLOOD AND ASHES ISBN 0-922356-25-4
19. FIRESTORM IN BABYLON ISBN 0-922356-27-0
20. THE MOSSAD CONNECTION ISBN 0-922356-28-9
21. CREATION, THE SACRED UNIVERSE ISBN 1-56935-047-7
23. BURNT OFFERINGS ISBN 0-922356-33-5
24. SHROUDS OF THE SEVENTH SEAL ISBN 0-922356-34-3

25. THE BITTER COMMUNION ISBN 0-922356-37-8
26. COUNTERFEIT BLESSINGS THE ANTI-CHRIST BY ANY NAME: KHAZARS ISBN 0-922356-36-6
27. PHOENIX OPERATOR-OWNER MANUAL ISBN 1-56935-018-3
28. OPERATION SHANSTORM ISBN 0-922356-39-4
29. END OF THE MASQUERADE ISBN 0-922356-40-8
38. THE DARK CHARADE ISBN 0-922356-53-X
39. THE TRILLION DOLLAR LIE THE HOLOCAUST VOL. I ISBN 0-922356-55-6
40. THE TRILLION DOLLAR LIE THE HOLOCAUST VOL. II ISBN 0-922356-56-4
41. THE DESTRUCTION OF A PLANET ZIONISM *IS* RACISM ISBN 0-922356-60-2
42. UNHOLY ALLIANCE ISBN 0-922356-61-0
43. TANGLED WEBS VOL. I ISBN 0-922356-62-9
44. TANGLED WEBS VOL. II ISBN 0-922356-63-7
45. TANGLED WEBS VOL. III ISBN 0-922356-64-5
46. TANGLED WEBS VOL. IV ISBN 0-922356-65-3
48. TANGLED WEBS VOL. V ISBN 0-922356-68-8
49. TANGLED WEBS VOL. VI ISBN 0-922356-69-6
50. DIVINE PLAN VOL. I ISBN 1-56935-29-9
51. TANGLED WEBS VOL. VII ISBN 0-922356-81-5
52. TANGLED WEBS VOL. VIII ISBN 0-922356-83-1
53. TANGLED WEBS VOL. IX ISBN 0-922356-84-X
54. THE FUNNEL'S NECK ISBN 0-922356-86-6
55. MARCHING TO ZION ISBN 0-922356-87-4
56. SEX AND THE LOTTERY ISBN 0-922356-88-2
57. GOD'S PLAN 2000! DIVINE PLAN VOL. II ISBN 1-56935-028-0
58. FROM THE FRYING PAN INTO THE PIT OF FIRE ISBN 0-922356-90-4
59. "REALITY" ALSO HAS A DRUMBEAT ISBN 0-922356-91-2
60. AS THE BLOSSOM OPENS ISBN 0-922356-92-0
61. PROGRAMMING PITFALLS ISBN 1-56935-001-9
62. CHAPARRAL SERENDIPITY ISBN 1-56935-000-0

63. THE BEST OF TIMES ISBN 1-56935-002-7
64. TO ALL MY CHILDREN ISBN 1-56935-003-5
65. THE LAST GREAT PLAGUE ISBN 1-56935-004-3
66. ULTIMATE PSYCHOPOLITICS ISBN 1-56935-005-1
67. THE BEAST AT WORK ISBN 1-56935-006-X
68. ECSTASY TO AGONY ISBN 1-56935-007-8
69. TATTERED PAGES ISBN 1-56935-009-4
70. NO THORNLESS ROSES ISBN 1-56935-010-8
71. COALESCENCE ISBN 1-56935-012-4
72. CANDLELIGHT ISBN 1-56935-013-2
73. RELATIVE CONNECTIONS VOL. I ISBN 1-56935-016-7
74. MYSTERIES OF RADIANCE RELATIVE CONNECTIONS VOL. II ISBN 1-56935-019-1
75. TRUTH AND CONSEQUENCES REL. CONNECT. VOL. III ISBN 1-56935-020-5
76. SORTING THE PIECES REL. CONNECT. VOL. IV ISBN 1-56935-021-3
77. PLAYERS IN THE GAME ISBN 1-56935-022-1
78. IRON TRAP AROUND AMERICA ISBN 1-56935-023-X
79. MARCHING TO ZOG ISBN 1-56935-024-8
80. TRUTH FROM THE "ZOG BOG" ISBN 1-56935-025-6
81. RUSSIAN ROULETTE AMONG OTHER THINGS ISBN 1-56935-026-4
82. RETIREMENT RETREATS OR WHICH CONCENTRATION CAMP DO YOU PREFER? ISBN 1-56935-027-2
83. POLITICAL PSYCHOS ISBN 1-56935-030-2
84. CHANGING PERSPECTIVES ISBN 1-56935-031-0
85. SHOCK THERAPY FOR A BRAIN DEAD WORLD ISBN 1-56935-032-9
86. MISSING THE LIFEBOAT?? ISBN 1-56935-033-7
87. IN GOD'S NAME AWAKEN ISBN 1-56935-034-5
88. ADVANCED DEMOLITION LEGION (THE ADL IN ACTION) ISBN 1-56935-035-3
89. FOCUS OF DEMONS ISBN (REAL GREMLINS IN THE WORKS) 1-56935-037-X
90. TAKING OFF THE BLINDFOLD ISBN 1-56935-038-8

91. FOOTSTEPS INTO TRUTH *UNCOVERING LIES AND FRAUD ABOUT GOD AND MAN* ISBN 1-56935-039-6
92. WALK THE CROOKED ROAD WITH THE CROOKS ISBN 1-56935-040-X
93. CRIMINAL POLITBUROS AND OTHER PLAGUES ISBN 1-56935-041-8
94. WINGING IT... ISBN 1-56935-044-2
95. HEAVE-UP (PHASE ONE) ISBN 1-56935-046-9
96. HEAVE-HO (PHASE TWO) ISBN 1-56935-048-5
97. HEAVE 'EM OUT (PHASE THREE, PART 1) ISBN 1-56935-049-3
98. ASCENSION OR NEVER-EVER LAND ISBN 1-56935-050-7
99. USURPERS OF FREEDOM IN CONSPIRACY ISBN 1-56935-051-5
100. BUTTERFLIES, MIND CONTROL--THE RAZOR'S EDGE IT'S ALL IN THE GAME ISBN 1-56935-052-3

GOA. THE GARDEN OF ATON by Nora Boyles
ISBN 1-56935-011-6 $6.00 plus $2.50 S&H

FOR INFORMATION OR ORDERS CALL:
1-800-800-5565

PHOENIX SOURCE DISTRIBUTORS, Inc.
P.O. Box 27353
Las Vegas, Nevada 89126

<u>MASTERCARD, VISA OR DISCOVER CARDS</u>

What Are The Phoenix Journals?

Many people have asked us what the *PHOENIX JOURNALS* are. They contain the true history (His-story) of mankind on this planet as well as detailed information about the most asked about and wondered about subjects (i.e., Spirituality, E.T.s, our origin, our purpose here on this planet, etc.). Commander Hatonn and the other Higher Spiritual Teachers who have authored these *JOURNALS*, weave spiritual lessons and insights throughout the unveiling of lies which have been deceptively forced upon us, throughout time, by the Elite anti-Christ controllers. These *JOURNALS* are the "*DEAD SEA SCROLLS*" of our time. Their importance in the growth of mankind cannot be overstated. They are the textbooks of understanding which God promised us we would have, to guide us through the "End Times".

Here is what Commander Hatonn has said about the *PHOENIX JOURNALS*. Quoting from *JOURNAL* #40, THE TRILLION DOLLAR LIE, Vol.II, pgs. 47 & 48: "Some day in the far recesses of the future experiences of another human civilization—these *JOURNALS* will be found and TRUTH will again be given unto the world manifest so that another lost civilization can regain and find its way. God always gives His creations that which they need when the sequence is proper. It is what man DOES WITH THESE THINGS which marks the civilization. WHAT WILL YOUR LEGACY BE????? I focus on current activities which might turn your world about in time to save your ecosystems and your sovereignty as nations and peoples. You cannot wait to be filled in on the lies of the generations lest you wait until too late to take control of your circumstance presently within the lies. YOU ARE A PEOPLE OF MASSIVE DECEPTION AND WHAT YOU WILL DO WITH THIS INFORMATION IN ACTION DETERMINES YOUR PURPOSE AND GROWTH IN THIS WONDROUS MANIFESTED EXPERIENCE—WILL YOU PERISH PHYSICALLY OF THE EVIL INTENT, OR WILL YOU MOVE INTO AND WITHIN THE PLACES OF HOLY CREATOR? THE CHOICE IS YOURS."

In case you didn't know, Phoenix Source Distributors, Inc. can automatically send you the latest *PHOENIX JOURNALS* as they are printed. This gives you an extra discount on new *JOURNALS* and you don't have to keep remembering to order. Call (800) 800-5565 for details.

See Back Page for ordering information.

Brent Moorhead
Business Manager

ARE YOU UP TO DATE WITH KEY ISSUES?

Learn The Truth Behind What You're Being Told

PHOENIX JOURNALS *BONUS SELECTION* OFFER

Choose from the following *BONUS SELECTION* offers and save!

Bonus Selection 'A' Single copy *Bonus* price $6.00 ea. (Was $7.95)
Bonus Selection 'B' Any 4 Journals—*Bonus* price $5.50 ea. (Save $2.00)
Bonus Selection 'C' 10 or more Journals—*Bonus* price $5.00 ea. (Save $10)

Shipping and handling extra (see order form for rates). Credit Cards, Check or Money Order accepted. Complete the order form found in this section, enclose payment and mail. Please allow 30 days for delivery.

AND THEY CALLED HIS NAME IMMANUEL— I AM SANANDA
BY SANANDA & JUDAS ISCARIOTH
#2 $6.00   156 Pages

The story of the life of the one known as Jesus of Nazareth (Immanuel) is told by Jesus and his disciple and scribe, Judas Iscarioth. Judas' name is cleared and the actual one who betrayed Immanuel is revealed. Clarification is given concerning Immanuel's life and teachings, such as: The Purpose Of His Life—His 40 Days With Cosmic Beings—His Crucifixion, Resurrection And His Journey After Resurrection—Clarification Regarding God, The Creation, The Laws And Commandments. (INDEX INCLUDED)

THE RAINBOW MASTERS
BY THE MASTERS
#7 $6.00 150 Pages

This JOURNAL is a manual for living the life blessed of God. Cuts to the core of the nature of man, yet offers gentle direction filled with compassion beyond measure. Each energy is uniquely powerful, yet, together they form a team of one. The Masters offer insight to the planet, our purpose, God's involvement and will, our journey home, the Greater Vision. The messages resonate as musical chords within the very soul essence. The words shared renew hope and give the phrase "Trust in God" a deeper meaning. (INDEX INCLUDED)

PHOENIX OPERATOR-OWNER MANUAL
BY SANANDA, MICHAEL, GERMAIN & HATONN
#27 $6.00   114 Pages

This JOURNAL is GOD's deliverance of Truth to YOU, His blinded fledgling creatures. HE is offering YOU the instructions for reaching the 'Lighted' Path back home to HIM, AND THUS TO ONENESS. You will learn HOW to recognize the Anti-Christ, (that which is AGAINST GOD and therefore AGAINST LIFE) within you and why, through your gift of free-will, YOU allowed the Anti-Christ within your temple of God. You will learn about: The "Deadliest" Sins (Errors), Personal Responsibility For Consequences And Experiences. (INDEX INCLUDED)

THROUGH DARKNESS INTO LIGHT
THE DIVINE PLAN—VOL. I
BY GYEORGOS CERES HATONN-ATON
#50 $6.00   261 Pages

Hatonn writes about various subjects such as: The Importance Of Atlantis And Lemuria In Our History—The Philippine Islands And Their Key Part In Ancient History And Immediate Future—The Truth About The Birthing Of Planet Earth & Our Moon, Plus History Of The Outer Planets In Ancient Sumarian Texts—History Of The Photon Belt, Its Cycle And Significance—Walter Stickney, United States Dictator-In-Waiting (FEMA)—Masonic Symbols In The Washington, D.C. Street Layout.   (INDEX INCLUDED)

GOD, TOO, HAS A PLAN 2000!
DIVINE PLAN—VOL. II
BY GYEORGOS CERES HATONN
57 $6.00   237 Pages

Some of the very important topics covered are: THE SUMARIANS, A LOST CIVILIZATION—Excerpts From Pontius Pilote's Report—Creation/Creationists—Capture Theory Of The Moon—CHRIST WAS NOT A JEW—Three Phases Of Earth's Cleansing—HICRV: Deadly New Virus—Freemasonry And The "Mark of The Beast"—POW/MIAs—Banking Maneuvers—Nebuchadnezzar's Dream—Freemasonry Doctrines—The Weavers—Recent Earthquakes—Storms—More Elite Plans.   (INDEX INCLUDED)

PHOENIX JOURNALS *BONUS SELECTION* ORDER FORM
BONUS SELECTION OFFER

Choose from the following *BONUS SELECTION* offers and save!

Bonus Selection 'A' Single copy *Bonus* price $6.00 ea. (Was $7.95)
Bonus Selection 'B' Any 4 Journals—*Bonus* price $5.50 ea. (Save $2.00)
Bonus Selection 'C' 10 or more Journals—*Bonus* price $5.00 ea. (Save $10)

TITLE	QUANITY	PRICE	TOTAL

SHIPPING CHARGES:

USA (except Alaska & Hawaii)
UPS-$3.75 1st title, $1.00 each add'l
Bkrate-$2.50 1st title, $1.00 each add'l
Priority-$3.40 1st title, $1.00 ea add'l

ALASKA & HAWAII
Bkrate-$2.50 1st title, $1.00 ea add'l
Priority-$3.40 1st title, $1.00 ea add'l
UPS 2Day-$9.00 1st title, $1.00 ea add'l

CANADA & MEXICO
Surface-$3.00 1st title, $1.50 ea add'l
Air Book-$4.50 1st title, $2.00 ea add'l

FOREIGN
Surface-$3.00 1st title, $1.50 ea add'l
Air Book-$8.00 per title estimate

Phoenix Journal Total _____
Shipping (please circle one)
UPS   PRIORITY   BOOKRATE   AIRBOOK   SURFACE   OTHER
SUBTOTAL _____
Nevada Residents add 7% Sales Tax _____
TOTAL ENCLOSED _____

Name_____

Address_____

City, State & Zip_____
Tel:( ) _____ Credit Card #: _____
Expiration date_____ Signature_____

Allow 30 days for delivery. We accept Visa, MasterCard and Discover.
All payments in U.S. Funds to:
**Phoenix Source Distributors, Inc. P.O. Box 27353 Las Vegas, NV 89126
800-800-5565 Call For Availability.**

TAPES, TRANSCRIPTIONS & VIDEOS

THE WORD NOW ACCEPTS VISA, DISCOVER AND MASTER CARDS

In addition to audio tapes of meetings with Commander Hatonn, THE WORD is now offering written transcriptions of some taped topics. Donations to cover the costs of tapes are $4.00 for one tape, $6.00 for two tapes and $2.50 **per tape** for three or more. The transcriptions are $3.00 each. (Mexico or Canada add $0.25 and other foreign countries add $0.50 per tape or transcription.) Please send check or money order to: *THE WORD*, **P.O. Box 6194, Tehachapi, CA 93582. Call 805-822-4176** if you have questions or you wish to use your credit card.

If you desire to automatically receive tapes from future meetings, please send at least a $50 donation from which tape costs will be deducted. We will try to notify you as your balance reaches zero.

Special Order tapes are noted below by * and are **not** automatically sent since this material is either already in print or will be soon. Available written transcriptions are noted by #.

The following is a complete list of meeting dates with the number of tapes **in bold** in parentheses and mentioning if the meeting has a special focus:

4/25/92**(2)***# "The Photon Belt";
5/11/92**(3)*** "Silent Weapons For Quiet Wars";
5/30/92**(3)*** "The Divine Plan and Places In Between" tapes 1-3;
6/30/92**(3)*** "The Divine Plan and Places In Between" tapes 4-6;
7/4/92**(2)** radio program, KTKK, Salt Lake City, UT;
7/12/92**(3)**;
7/18/92**(2)** radio program, KTKK, Salt Lake City, UT;
7/26/92**(3)**.
8/3/92**(2)** radio program, KTKK, Salt Lake City, UT;
8/8/92**(2)**
8/16/92**(3)*** Bo Gritz speech in Tehachapi
8/16/92**(1)** **VIDEO TAPE (**Bo Gritz' complete speech in Tehachapi) **Special order only**, $12
8/31/92**(2)*** "Anti-Christ Banksters"
9/5/92**(2)**;

1

9/9/92(2) radio program KTKK
9/12/92(2) radio KTKK
10/4/92(3) meeting
10/10/92(2) meeting
10/17/92(2) radio KTKK
10/24/92(2); 11/1/92(2)
11/1/92(1) radio program, New Mexico;
11/8/92(2); 11/14/92(3); 11/22/92(2); 11/29/92(2)
12/6/92(2); 12/13/92(2); 12/20/92(2)
12/7/92(2) Cosmos Patriot Group I;
12/8/92(1) Cosmos Patriot Group II;
12/12/92(2) Cosmos Patriot Group III;
12/13/92(2); 12/20/92(2); 1/2/93(2)
12/31/92(1)* Constitutional Law Center
1/14/93(2) Seminar speech by retired Police Officer Jack McLamb;
1/16/93(2); 1/23/93(3); 1/30/93(2); 2/6/93(1); 2/13/93(2);
2/18/93(2); 2/20/93(2); radio program on KTKK featuring Soltec with Hatonn.
4/4/93(3) including Soltec and Sananda.
4/10/93(2) radio program KTKK
4/24/93(3); 5/2/93(2); 5/16/93(2); 5/23/93(3); 6/20/93(2).
6/20/93(1)* mystery virus in N. Mexico.
7/2/93(2)* Rayelan Russbacher on KTKK;
7/31/93(1) KTKK Little Crow.
7/11/93(3); 7/18/93(2); 7/30/93(2); 8/8/93(2);
8/21/93(2); 8/22/93(3) Gunther Russbacher inteview.
8/29/93(2): 9/14/93(2); 9/19/93(3); 10/9/93(3); 10/16/93(3);
10/30/93(2); 11/13/93(2); 11/21/93(3); 11/27/93(2); 12/5/93(2);
12/12/93(2); 12/18/93(1); 1/8/94(2); 1/16/94(2); 1/23/94(2);
2/7/94(2); 2/13/94(4); 3/6/94(2); 4/3/94(1); 4/17/94(2);
5/1/94(2); 5/8/94(2), Mothers' Day; 5/14/94(3); 5/29/94(2);
6/18/94(2); 7/3/94(3); 7/24/94(2); 7/26/94(2); 7/31/94(2;
8/6/94(2); 8/14/94(2); 8/28/94(2); 9/11/94(2); 9/25/94(2);
10/10/94(5) Columbus Day; 10/28 & 30(4); 11/6/94(2);
11/20/94(2); 11/27/94(2); 12/11/94(2); 12/18/94(2); 1/8/94(2);
1/15/95(3) Norio Hayakawa & Jordan Maxwell; 1/22/95(2);
2/5/95(2); 2/10/95(3) meeting with Japanese visitors and Jordan Maxwell; 2/19/95(4) Jordan Maxwell Lecture
#1-#5 Corporation Lectures ($5 each tape.)

THE WORD, P.O. Box 6194, Tehachapi, CA 93582. 805-822-4176
VISA, DISCOVER AND MASTER CARDS ACCEPTED